The
Dark Side
of
Nowhere

ALSO BY NEAL SHUSTERMAN:

Speeding Bullet
The Eyes of Kid Midas
What Daddy Did
The Shadow Club
Dissidents
Scorpion Shards
Darkness Creeping
Darkness Creeping II
Mindquakes
Mindstorms

The Dark Side of Nowhere

A Novel by

NEAL SHUSTERMAN

Little, Brown and Company

Boston   New York   Toronto   London

First Edition

Library of Congress Cataloging-in-Publication Data

Shusterman, Neal.
    The dark side of nowhere : a novel / by Neal Shusterman. — 1st ed.
        p.   cm.
    Summary: Fourteen-year-old Jason faces an identity crisis after discovering that he is the son of aliens who stayed on Earth following a botched invasion mission.
    ISBN 0-316-78907-0
    [1. Extraterrestrial beings — Fiction.   2. Identity — Fiction.   3. Science fiction.]   I. Title.
PZ7.S55987Dap   1997
[Fic] — dc20   96-19895

10 9 8 7 6 5 4 3

MV – NY

Published simultaneously in Canada
by Little, Brown & Company (Canada) Limited

Printed in the United States of America

ACKNOWLEDGMENTS

I'd like to thank the teachers and librarians who read the earliest drafts of this novel and helped bring it from the dark side into the light of day: Jeanne Hess, Roz Finnegan, David Nelson, Judy Cowart, Darcy Stepka, Linda Powley, Pamela Carroll, and Sarah Nix. Many thanks to the Fictionaires, whose insightful suggestions helped to mold the book chapter by chapter. My love and thanks to Elaine, Brendan, and Jarrod, for always being there to remind me of the really important things, and to Lloyd Segan and Devra Lieb, for seeing the possibilities. Last, my deepest gratitude goes to John Keller, who took this project under his wing and made it a reality.

This book is dedicated to the memory of all those who have died at the hands of the warrior-fools. . . .

1

Nowhere Fast

Ethan died of a burst appendix.

That's what we were told — and we had no reason to doubt it. Everyone on the street had heard the way he screamed. The pain must have been unbearable. Even after his parents had rushed him off to the hospital, his screams haunted me for days.

We found out about it the next morning.

It was during science class. We were studying the astronomers, and somewhere between Copernicus and Galileo, the announcement came hissing over the loudspeaker. It was a shock — biggest one I could remember. I mean, in this day and age, to keel over from something as stupid as appendicitis. I couldn't look over at his empty seat that morning. Although I tried to feel sad, all I could feel was angry.

Roxanne, the last in a long line of girlfriends that had filled Ethan's seventh- and eighth-grade years, was blubbering away. That made me angry, too. I noticed the way she rubbed those eyes as she wailed, purposely smudging her mother's mascara that she always wore. It made her tears thick and black, so everyone could see from a mile away how very *sad* she was — as if everyone should feel sorry for her, and not Ethan.

On the other hand, Paula Quinn cried silent tears that she quickly wiped away. It was classy. It was *real*. I watched Paula rather than look at Ethan's seat or watch Roxanne's Cavalcade of Misery.

In front of the room, Mr. Smith, our science teacher, spoke in solemn tones, using an all-knowing, all-comforting voice that he must have borrowed from Pastor Bob, our minister.

"We'll all miss Ethan," he said, "but we have to remember that he's gone to a better place."

Next to me, my friend Wesley flicked his hair back in utter contempt — a gesture he had learned from me — then he whispered under his breath, "Better place? I'll bet."

Up front, Mr. Smith lifted his eyes upward, as if searching for heaven in the flickering fluorescents. "Let us all observe a moment of silence in Ethan's memory."

I flicked my own hair back contemptuously, showing Wesley how it was done.

"Moment of silence, my butt," I whispered to Wes. "Ethan would have wanted a moment of heavy metal."

That made Wes snicker. It sounded so rudely loud in the silence that it made me snicker, too, and my snicker set someone off on the other side of the room.

It wasn't like this was funny or anything — but sometimes, when something hits you so hard, your head kind of starts ricocheting off every wall. Suddenly laughter and tears feel like the same thing.

More chuckles broke out around the room. Mr. Smith threw

me a cold warning look, as if it were all my fault. "Jason . . . ," he said, "don't you dare."

Then Roxanne turned to us with her raccoon eyes and wailed, "What's wrong with you people!"

That did it. The raccoon eyes, Smith's fluorescent gaze, and a dead friend. It was all so unreal, some confused part of our brains concluded that it must have been funny. Half the room burst out in snickers punctuated by sobs. Then my own brain took a bad ricochet, and I suddenly felt like heaving, so I burst out of the room, fighting to keep my breakfast from making a surprise appearance.

"Mr. Miller!" Smith shouted after me, but I was already out the door, with Wesley following close behind.

I stopped when I reached the water fountain in the hallway, and bent down to take a drink, hoping to drown my gut into submission. Wesley punched a locker hard enough to make it rattle, but not hard enough to hurt himself. It's a show, I thought, just like Smith. Just like Roxanne. I didn't want to put on a show, so I drank from the fountain and I didn't say a thing.

"This sucks," said Wes, meaning everyone and everything. "What a lousy way to end the ninth grade, you know?"

As I stood up from the water fountain, Paula Quinn came up behind Wes. She was red in the face. No longer from crying — it was because she was angry. Angry like me.

"I just want you to know that what you did in there stunk, Jason," she said, staring me down with furious eyes. "You're real creeps, you know that?"

I could have just shrugged it off, or yelled back at her, or said something cold and clever. The thing is I just couldn't do

3

that to Paula. We weren't like friends or anything. Although I did ask her out once. She turned me down. Ever since then, it's been kind of weird between her and me. Like I respect her or something.

"I didn't mean to laugh," I told her. "I don't know why I did, and I feel lousy about it, okay?"

She looked at me, and I guess she read some honesty in my face, because she didn't seem as mad anymore. "Were you and Ethan friends from the time you were little?"

I nodded. Kids didn't come and go from Billington very often. Not that we didn't want to, but our parents had roots like oak trees — they wouldn't dream of moving away. So most of us knew each other all our lives. Ethan, Wesley, and I were a famous threesome. The Trilogy of Terror, our teachers used to call us.

Paula, on the other hand, was a newcomer, having just landed in Billington four months ago. She was a pleasant glimpse of the world most of us only got to see on TV.

"You know what really gets me?" I said. "It's that Ethan's whole life began and ended in this poor excuse for a town. It's pathetic. I don't want to remember Ethan as being pathetic."

"He wasn't pathetic," said Paula. "And this town's not so bad anyway."

"Yeah," I said, "wait until *you've* been here for fourteen years — then we'll see how you feel about it."

Then came a voice from behind us — a deep voice, that boomed even when speaking in hushed tones.

"Ethan's not dead," said the voice. We turned to see Mr. Grant, who was the security guard and janitor at Billington Junior High. Grant was kind of an odd guy — a loner who never

said much to any of us but always seemed to know everyone's business. His words made us all hang on the moment, not knowing whether he was kidding or knew something we didn't.

"He's not dead, as long as we remember him," he said, and then laughed — not just a chuckle but a deep belly laugh, like something was uproariously funny. It was far more inappropriate than my laughter had been. Well, I figured, what should we expect from a guy whose motto was "I'll clean this school up one way or another."

His laughter faded, and he scratched his reddish blond beard, which was always so neatly trimmed. "You belong in class," he reminded us. "I suggest you get going." Then he turned and walked off, his large key ring jingling from his belt like a psychotic wind chime.

As we made our way back toward class, Paula whispered into my ear, "That was too weird." Turns out she was right.

If God threw a dart at the world and it happened to strike Billington, completely obliterating it, no one would notice and no one would care. In fact, I often thought it would be the best thing that could happen to this place. Smack in the middle of the state, Billington is on a highway that couldn't be straighter if you drew it with a ruler, and whenever I heard people talk about going nowhere fast, I figured they were headed here, although I couldn't see what the hurry would be. We've got your typical fast-food places, an uninspired mall, and way too many satellite dishes — because in a place like this, what else is there to do but watch five hundred channels of TV? If boredom was a living, breathing thing, then its less interesting cousin would live in Billington.

My parents didn't mind a nowhere sort of life. It seemed to me that their universe began and ended in Billington. All you had to do was spend a few microseconds looking through our house to get a good clue about my parents. For instance, they had this book of Norman Rockwell art that sat out on the coffee table like a slab of granite. Norman Rockwell painted goofy-looking people doing dull, everyday things. My parents had whole collections of boring art books and prints — like the woman who sat out in a wheat field, and the farmer with his pitchfork and his disgusted-looking wife. Mom and Dad called it their Americana Collection. I called it their Anesthesia Collection, because if I looked at it long enough, it would render me unconscious.

Then there was dinner conversation. Sitting at the table with my parents was like purgatory, because conversation in the Miller household was always the same, even when they used different words.

"Mary, this chicken is wonderful."

"I got the recipe from Jenny down the street."

"We'll have to invite them over for dinner. We'll have a barbecue."

"That would be nice."

One time, in the middle of their drivel, I slammed the ketchup bottle on the table, sending a stream of ketchup rocketing against the ceiling.

"What's wrong with you?" I screamed at them. "Why can't you argue and fight, and do things like *normal* people?"

Mom was miffed by the ketchup on the ceiling — which was part of the problem. All she ever got was "miffed." She never got furious; she never picked up something breakable and threw it across the room; she never said something to me that she'd feel sorry for later, no matter how much I deserved it. Her keel was about as even as a ship in a bottle.

"I'm sorry we can't be a little more dysfunctional for you," she told me in her classic miffed tone as she handed me a mop to clean the ketchup from the ceiling. "Would you be happier if we beat you and locked you in the closet?"

"Won't know until you try," I said snidely. Dad promptly issued a punishment for the evening's disrespect. No computer games for three days. Although I complained bitterly, I had to admit, the punishment was fair. It always was.

As far as being dysfunctional, well, I tried. I read enough books and saw enough TV shows about dysfunctional families to get down the basics, but I could never seem to make it stick. It pissed me off, because I never had a real decent reason to be angry at Mom and Dad. They didn't mistreat me; they didn't go on drinking binges; Dad didn't have a girlfriend on the side. Nothing. I did give them plenty of reasons to be angry at *me*, though. I would spend endless hours trying to invent some sort of drama in our lives — suspensions from school, fights with other kids, a bag of oregano that I told everyone was pot. I even sprayed some rude graffiti on the side of our house once, figuring it might get us in the local paper and make for an interesting couple of days. But Dad painted it over before anyone saw, and didn't bother to report it. Once the school counselor suggested that we all go in for some family therapy — and I thought I had won some minor victory. But after the third session, the therapist concluded that we were hopelessly well adjusted.

After so much torturous normalcy, almost anything would

have been a welcome relief. But it's kind of sick when the death of a friend is the only exciting thing you can point to in recent history.

There was a big turnout for Ethan's funeral. I guess everyone in town knew Ethan's family, because his parents were real estate agents and their faces were on notepads in everyone's kitchens. In Billington, that was the closest you could get to being famous. The day left me feeling weird for a whole lot of reasons I was still trying to figure out. Although everything went the way it was supposed to go, something inside me kept saying that it wasn't a normal funeral. And believe me, I know normal.

That night, I sat with my dad in the garage, for once not minding the boredom of home.

"Hand me the hammer, son."

My dad talked like an old Andy Griffith rerun. I refused to ever call him Pa.

"Dad," I said as I handed him the tool, "why do you think Ethan's parents didn't cry?" I was as interested in how he would react to the question as I was in the answer. The fact was, not only didn't Ethan's parents cry, but they kept shifting their feet and checking their watches, as if this was little more than a real estate deal they wanted to close.

Even stranger to me, however, was how Dad seemed to be acting now. My father had about three emotions. Worry never seemed to be one of them, but now he wrinkled his brow with a look of concern that didn't sit right with me. I thought that it might be just a reaction from his monthly shots, but I knew he hadn't had them yet — we both were scheduled to get our shots at the same time, next Monday.

He thought about his answer, and then just tried to shrug it off.

"Shock," he said. "Simple shock."

But there was something more. It had to do with the worry on his face. He said no more, just returned to the bureau he was building for the Carters. He always put his full attention on his woodworking. That was probably why his work was so good. But today his attention was elsewhere, because he caught the edge of his finger with the hammer.

He shouted a word that I rarely heard him use, although, I must admit that I use it on a regular basis. Hearing him say it made me smile. "Dad," I said, "we're gonna have to wash that trash-mouth out with soap."

Dad chuckled through his gritted teeth and held his thumb until the pain subsided. Then he turned to me and took a good look — the way only a father does. He took in every feature, memorizing my face, as if he might never see it again. I thought I knew what he was thinking.

"Dad," I said, feeling a bit embarrassed, "come on — I'm not gonna get appendicitis or anything."

"No," he said. "No, you won't. We won't let that happen."

I chuckled at how weird he sounded, and began to feel cold — not on the outside, but on the inside, as if I was stuck neck-deep in the tip of an iceberg . . . and I had the feeling that this iceberg went clear down to China.

2

The Bleacher Brawl

I guess when you think about it, lots of small towns are like their own universes. Small events seem big, and big events in the outside world seem unimportant, because they're so far away. It was hard to imagine anything we did in our own corner of nowhere ever having an effect on the world. But sometimes huge things can take root in unexamined corners. I can pretty safely say that what happened in Billington never happened anywhere else on earth. At least I hope it didn't. But up till now we were all clueless about it, and the clues didn't start coming until Ethan's "appendicitis."

The first major clue came, of all places, at a Little League game — and for a guy who spent most of his time reaching for a ticket out of Billington boredom, I was pretty unprepared when the ticket got jammed into my palm.

The people of Billington are Little League fanatics — it's like a religion to most folks here. When our teams played teams from out of town, you never heard the other towns cheering as much as our parents did. It was downright embarrassing. This week, however, everything started off a bit muted. You could say that Ethan's ghost was haunting the first inning — to be honest, his ghost was everywhere that first week. You never realize the holes a person leaves behind until you fall into them. At the start of the game, there was a big-deal ceremony, retiring Ethan's number. But by the second inning, nobody seemed to care that the Billington Bullets had a new first baseman. I guess some holes get paved over pretty quick.

Now, to set the record straight, I fouled out of Little League early on — much to my parents' dismay. The coach said my attitude was divisive to the team, which was fine by me. As far as I was concerned, Billington Little League was just one more example of the suffocating air of pleasantness that surrounded the town like an eternal silver lining, without a black cloud to go with it. After my quick exit from Little League, I spent my Saturday mornings vegging in front of the TV, playing channel roulette with the five hundred cartoons that our satellite dish dragged from the sky.

This season, however, had made a spectator out of me. I had my reasons.

It was early June, and already hot and balmy. I sat in the stands with Wesley, and about two dozen proud Billingtonites. I kept my eye on the pitcher.

"Where did she learn to throw a ball like that?" Wesley said after Paula Quinn had struck out her second batter.

"I guess she brought it with her from New Jersey," I answered.

"Think all the girls in New Jersey are like that?" asked Wesley.

I just shrugged, not caring to waste my energy answering a question that dumb.

I heard about the day Paula tried out for the team. No one believed that a girl would be able to outpitch Billy Chambers, who was then the king of the mound, but she showed them real quick. Then, right after she had turned poor Billy into a relief pitcher, she asked him out to the movies.

That was class, because you have to understand one thing — Billy Chambers, aside from being the second-best pitcher Billington had ever seen, was about as butt-ugly as is legally allowed. Not even his Little League stardom could change that. On top of it, he was an angry kid, too, and ugly multiplied by angry equaled zero social life. So here, in the moment of his absolute humiliation, the pretty new girl who had just booted him to the bull pen was asking him for a date. Suddenly his humiliation didn't seem that bad after all. In fact, he probably thought he planned it that way. Of course they didn't go to more than two movies together before there were other girls who wanted some of Billy's moose-faced attention, too. So Billy broke up with her and went off to play the eighth-grade field.

As an observer, I realized that this is what Paula had intended all along. Sheer brilliance, and almost as skillful as her curveball. Yeah, she was definitely different from most of the kids in Billington.

I was dreaming about all the conversations Paula and I might have if she didn't hate my guts, when I heard the voice behind me.

If there's such a thing as intuition, I wasn't blessed with it. If there's such a thing as a premonition, I never had one — although I should have when I heard that voice. I should have seen lightning bolts and my whole life flashing before my eyes.

"How come you're not out there?" said the deep voice.

I couldn't place it at first. I didn't say anything back, because I didn't know he was talking to me. Actually he was talking to both Wesley and me.

I turned around to see Mr. Grant, our notorious security-janitor. Wesley replied first, with his typical shrug of an answer. "I don't know, maybe because I got a life?" he said, which was really just wishful thinking.

Grant stared straight at me. "So what's your excuse?"

"I used to play," I told him. "But I got allergic."

"I remember," he said, to my uncomfortable surprise.

"Why should you care?" I asked.

He took off his cap and scratched his thick blond hair. He wasn't an old man, but worn and weathered, the way cowboys are in the movies. He rubbed his beard thoughtfully. "A kid like you should develop his skills," he said. "Agility, reflexes, pinpoint accuracy. A kid like you is gonna need those skills."

By now that run-in that I had with him the other day was creeping back into my mind — that weird thing he said about Ethan. I was starting to get squirmy.

"Baseball and I do fine without each other."

He nodded and didn't say anything else, but still his voice rang within my head, and I swore I could feel his eyes burning into the back of my neck, right until the last inning.

That's when I got into the fight with the big kid one row down.

It was stupid, really. Maybe it was because I was hot, or maybe because Grant had gotten under my skin in a way I couldn't fathom, but then again, maybe it was just because I couldn't stomach morons. Anyway, these two kids were rooting for the other team — which was fine, but one of them kept whispering rude things about Paula beneath his breath, as if calling her names would somehow change the no-hitter she was throwing.

I imagined this guy was an insect beneath my feet, and so I planted my foot firmly on his hand, which was resting on the bench.

"Hey, what's your problem?" he said.

"Sorry," I told him. "I mistook you for a cockroach. Easy mistake."

By now, Wesley, who had a stronger survival instinct than I did, began leaning away from me, pretending he didn't know me.

The guy, who was in high school and about three inches taller than me, lifted his tread-marked hand and whapped me in the stomach. So I whapped him in the face, and as the crowd cheered the first hit off of Paula, I dove headlong into a brawl.

It was no contest. I knew it was a lost cause from the beginning, but then lost causes were always my specialty. Turns out the guy was on the high-school kick-boxing team, so not only could he punch my lights out, but he could kick them out as well.

I got beat up so bad, the guy was embarrassed.

By now there was a crowd around me peering down in pity. That hurt worse than the beating.

"Are you okay, son?" some old guy said, like he was helping some snot-nosed kid on a playground.

"I'm fine," I said, not looking anyone in the face, "just fine." And I limped at full speed toward the restrooms across the park.

Once inside, I felt my guts wanting to view the world

14

through my open mouth, but I wouldn't let them. I told myself it was just the septic smell of the dank bathroom that made me feel that way, and I swallowed hard, forcing the feeling back down into my gut. Then I splashed cold water on my face and tried to deny that I was crying. I've always cried too often for a kid whose supposed to be a tough pain-in-the-ass. But no one ever sees. I reached for a towel to dry my face, but there were none, just one of those useless air blowers, and when I looked up, I caught my reflection in the mirror.

My lips were puffing up, my right eye was turning colors, and if that wasn't awful enough, I began to have one of those really miserable moments when you see more than just your reflection in the mirror. Past, present, and future. I saw me in all my glory. I felt all the anger from the fight coming back like a boomerang until it was focused on that reflection, swelling up, growing uglier than Billy Chambers.

It would have been so easy to stare at that reflection and scream at it, "I hate you," but I'd been through that before, enough to know that hating myself wasn't the problem or the solution. I didn't know what was wrong. I didn't know what I wanted — I just wanted. And all I knew for sure was that Billington was to blame. If I could wipe it, and every town like it, off the face of the planet, I would have done it without a second thought and without a stitch of remorse. But all I had the power to do was to hide in a urine-stenched bathroom, wishing it would all just go away.

The bathroom door opened behind me.

Then it closed.

I figured it was just someone coming in to take a leak, until I heard the voice.

"Your head's a mess and you don't know why."

This time I didn't have to turn around to know that it was Grant.

He continued, so sure of his words. "You have an instinct to fight, but there's nothing worth the battle. How sad for you." And then he left, letting the door swing closed behind him.

I went after him. Nobody reaches into my head like that without me retaliating with some serious verbal abuse.

I found him leaning up against the side of the cinder-block restroom, with a large brown paper bag at his feet.

"What the hell's your problem?" I spat out.

He shook his head. "Not my problem — yours."

"What do you know about it?"

"Enough," he said. Then he looked at me and grinned, like he was seeing right through me. "Your life is so pleasant. Everything about it is so *nice*."

He was right. "Nice" is exactly what it was. Not terrible, not wonderful; neither cold nor hot. Room temperature. Nice. A fouler word had never been invented.

"It's all so steady and so smooth," Grant continued. "You're afraid you'll live nice, then die nice, and your life will have been a nice waste of time. Am I right?"

I nodded.

"Well," he said, "it's not gonna happen that way."

I breathed a heavy sigh of relief — as if hearing him say it made it true — and I began to realize just how much power this man suddenly had over me. I wanted to know how he could have done that — but more important, I wanted to know why.

"You need excitement and worlds to conquer," he said with a knowing gleam in his eye. "Something you can *feel*."

16

There were alarms going off inside my head now. Suddenly this little cinder-block bathroom seemed miles from safety. I felt like a small child who didn't listen and took candy from the wrong stranger. *What did he want?*

Yet I could sense that this wasn't about something he wanted — it was about something he *knew*. Something about me, that nobody else was willing to tell. It thrilled me to think that there could be something about myself that I didn't already know, and the desire to know what it was muffled my alarms.

He picked up his crumpled grocery bag. Something heavy was inside. "Your parents have all chosen to forget," he said. "You have to make them remember."

By now the pain in my face and my bruised body seemed trivial. "What's in the bag?" I dared to ask him.

"It's for you," he said, handing it to me. "I believe it will fit."

I looked inside to see something metallic gray. It was a glove. A glove made of steel that went clear up to the elbow. It didn't look complicated — but it didn't look like something anyone around here had made.

"What am I supposed to do with this?" I asked.

Grant didn't answer me. Instead he said, "There's an old barn at the north end of Old Town Billington. Near where the bridge used to be. Be there Tuesday, after school. I'll show you how to use it."

"Old Town?" It was a long time since I heard the place even mentioned. It was a miserable corner of Billington, low on my list of places I'd ever care to visit again.

"Can I count on you?" he asked.

I wanted to ask him more questions, and yet all I could do was nod.

17

"Don't tell anyone," he said. "Don't show it to anyone." Then he strode off without looking back.

I ducked back into the bathroom, as if I had to hide the thing from the light of day, then I reached into the bag and pulled it out. It was clumsy and heavy — an unsightly thing with bulky ridges in unexpected places. Standing in front of the mirror, I slipped it on. It felt like it was made for a hand my size, but not necessarily a hand my shape. It seemed too flat and wide, still, when I moved my fingers, the fingers of the glove moved surprisingly easily.

Lifting my hand, I flexed my fingers, spreading them out as wide as they would go. And the mirror exploded.

3

Old Town

"Thanks for ruining my no-hitter yesterday," said Paula, standing in my doorway. "I'd punch you," she said, "but I don't think I could find a place left to bruise."

After my strange meeting with Grant the day before, I felt like someone had taken an eggbeater to my brain. Paula's appearance at my front door didn't help. Although my face wasn't as swollen as it had been, I still looked like a bad mug shot, so I tried to stand back in the afternoon shadows.

"What do you mean I ruined it?" I protested.

"You broke my concentration," she said.

"Try again — I didn't start fighting until *after* the ball got hit."

"No," said Paula, with the calm control of a prosecutor, "that creep was saying things about me, and you stepped on his hand. *That's* when I started throwing bad pitches."

"What are you, an alien? Do you have eyes in the back of your head?" I countered.

"No," she said, "but a pitcher has to be very observant."

Then it occurred to me that of all the people in the stands, she chose to be observant of me. The slightest grin came to my face — I couldn't hold it back. It made her uncomfortable — I could tell, because I'm pretty observant myself.

"Well," she said, "I just thought I'd tell you." Then she took a step back and turned to leave.

In that instant as she was turning away, I didn't have the chance to think about what I was going to say to keep her there. So I just shut down my brain and opened my mouth — which was a well-practiced talent of mine.

"There's something I want to show you," I said.

Paula turned back. "What?"

"Come on in." I opened the door, and she stepped in.

I led her through the house and out the back door, thankful that my parents were still at church and I was spared the burden of an explanation. Once out back, I reached under the back porch and pulled out the grocery bag Grant had given me.

"What are you doing?" asked Paula.

"You'll see."

Our backyard is almost an acre. You get yards that size when your town's in the boondocks. At the end of our property, there's a useless little barbed-wire fence, blocking off our land from the fallow pasture beyond, where no cows had grazed since before I was born.

I led Paula beneath the wire and over a hill, so neither my house nor any of the other homes on the road had a clear view of us.

Then I pulled the glove out of the bag and showed it to her.

"It's weird — what is it?" she asked.

"I'll show you."

About fifty yards away were a bunch of tin cans set up on old apple crates. I'd set them up myself the day before. I slipped

20

the glove on my hand, which was already becoming callused from wearing the clumsy thing. Then I pointed my index finger toward one of the cans . . . and tensed the muscle.

Fffft! Ping!

The can flew off the apple box. I was surprised that I got it on the first shot. It usually took nine or ten.

Paula looked at me uncertainly. "How'd you do that?"

I grinned. "It's magic," I said.

But she wasn't buying. "Nice try," she said, then grabbed my arm, turning it every which-way, practically breaking it off. She examined the fine, intricate device, from the pneumatic firing mechanism to the tiny barrels that spread across the back of my hand and to my fingertips like an exoskeleton. Then she found a catch near the elbow.

"No, don't!" I said — too late. She flipped it open, and the load of tiny ball bearings cascaded out, disappearing into the thick weeds of the meadow.

"Ha!" she announced. "I knew there was a rational explanation."

I knelt down, trying to salvage what BB's I could from the meadow. "You didn't have to do that," I whined — but shut up when I realized I was whining.

"So, it's a BB gun," she said.

"Well, yeah," I stammered, frustrated that she could reduce it to something so commonplace. "But it's a really cool BB gun. See, there are five channels — one running down the length of each finger. When you straighten your finger and tense it, it fires. You can fire in five different directions at the same time," I told her. "I could spread out my fingers and knock down five of those cans if I wanted to." Then, for emphasis,

I raised my hand, tensed my fingers, and sent five BB's flying simultaneously toward the row of cans. I missed them all.

Paula raised an eyebrow. "Who'd want to shoot in five different directions, anyway?"

"That's not the point," I explained, wishing she were a little more impressed. I slipped the glove off my hand and gave it to her, letting her feel its full weight. "You wanna try it?" I asked.

She didn't answer — she just looked at it, turning it over, taking in all its different angles and ridges.

"Jason," she finally said, "this is not normal."

My grin stretched wide "I know — isn't that great?"

I thought she might put it on, but she didn't. I was relieved. Just because I showed it to her didn't mean I was ready to share it.

"Where'd you get it?" she asked.

I hesitated. "I can't tell you that," I finally said.

Her face hardened. She was always honest; I suspect she wanted nothing less in return. "What's that supposed to mean?"

I realized I had already gone too far. I was supposed to keep it to myself. Tell no one. So I shrugged and gave no further answer.

I saw a gleam in her eye then, and the trace of a grin. I should have guessed what she was about to do, but like I said, intuition wasn't my strong point.

She turned and bolted, like she was sprinting for first base.

"Hey! Give that back!" I shouted.

She kept on running. "Not until you tell me where you got it."

I chased, barely able to keep up with her. I could hear her

laughing as she ran. At first I was laughing as well, but it got old real quick, when she didn't let me catch her.

We got farther and farther away from my house, running from field to field, climbing through wire fences, jumping over low, moss-covered stone walls. The trees got denser.

I knew the area behind my house pretty well, but there were some places that I just didn't go, and after playing this little game for ten minutes, I was so exhausted, I didn't know where I was headed.

Then we broke through a dense grove of oaks, and I saw the ruined remains of a storm-shattered house. I knew exactly where we were.

I stopped, refusing to chase Paula any farther. I put my hands on my knees, fighting to catch my breath.

Up ahead, Paula had stopped beside the abandoned house and was holding my glove over a stone opening in the ground — the entrance to an old storm cellar. Its steps led down into mossy darkness.

"So," she said, clearly threatening to drop it in, "tell me where you got it."

"We shouldn't be here," I told her. "Let's go."

"Not until you tell me," she said defiantly.

It made me angry to see her taunting me like that. Not wild-angry like I usually get, but angry in a way that focused my thoughts and made me know exactly what I wanted to say.

"I don't like you messing with my head," I told her, "and I don't like being treated like crap. If I can't tell you, then I've got a good reason — and if you can't accept that, then drop it in and leave."

She held the glove there for a second longer, then took it away from the hole.

"I thought you could take a joke," she said.

"I can take one," I told her, "but I won't *be* one."

She came over to me and gently put the glove back in my arms. "You're not," she said.

The moment could have turned uncomfortable then, if we both didn't have the good sense to look away from each other. She turned her attention to the ruined house behind us.

"I wonder who lived here."

"C'mon, let's get back," I said.

She looked at me, observing far more than I really wanted her to.

"You're spooked, aren't you?"

I would have denied it, but lying to Paula was still beyond my skill level. "This part of town gives me the creeps," I told her.

Telling her that was as good as an invitation.

She walked around to the front of the ruined house, for a moment putting aside thoughts of my BB glove, and I had no choice but to follow.

I found her standing in what was left of the front yard, staring at the street, her eyes rabbit-wide. "This is unreal!" she said.

Well, at least I had finally succeeded in impressing her.

The street before us — if you can call it a street — was weed-choked and broken into a mosaic of uneven asphalt. Trees lined the broken pavement. All dead. Skeletal hedges still clung to some of the pickets surrounding the homes. Some looked green, but the only thing living in them were the weeds that had tangled themselves up with the bushes.

Paula looked down the street, at a half dozen abandoned

homes on either side and the row of stores farther down. "What is this place?"

I pushed away a shiver and took hold of this golden opportunity to gain her undivided attention. "It's Old Town Billington," I told her. "Unluckiest place in the county." I sat on a tree stump as I wove the tale for her. "It started with a storm, about twenty years ago. A tornado ripped through the woods and took out this house — you can still see the path it cut." I pointed to the thin part of the woods. "Then, while people were still cleaning up, a bunch of 'em got the flu real bad. Some even died from it. That same year, when a blight started eating through the trees, people just gave up. I guess some got superstitious, and others couldn't stand the bad memories. Anyway, people moved to other parts of town, and when the bridge that led from here to the highway got washed out, there was no reason to rebuild it."

I looked around, trying to spot the old barn that Grant had mentioned. Even though the place seemed deserted, I was terrified he might be around, that he might see me flaunting my glove in front of Paula. I had to keep reminding myself that I never really promised him anything. Just because he asked me to keep it secret didn't mean I had to. Still, I slipped the glove underneath my shirt to keep it out of sight.

"So it's a real live ghost town," said Paula as we walked down the silent street. "In my old neighborhood, you don't get deserted houses. If a place gets deserted, they tear it down and build a strip mall. This is so strange."

Funny, but I never really thought of Old Town as being strange. I usually didn't think about it at all. It was kind of like that blind spot at the side of your eye. It's there, but who cares?

Like your appendix, I thought, but pushed that one out of my mind real quick.

"It's nothing special," I explained. "I mean, it wasn't exactly a center of activity. There's only this one street — then around the bend the homes thin out. There's only maybe thirty buildings in all."

"Do you ever come here, like with friends, to hang out?" she asked.

"When I was a kid," I said, "Wesley and I used to come here when we got bored. We'd throw rocks at the windows and stuff." I didn't tell Paula why we stopped coming here. The truth is, my father found out about it. It was the only time I ever saw him furious, the only time he ever hit me. A real old-fashioned spanking. Being that I was nine, and way too old for that sort of thing, I thought it would only hurt my pride, but, man, was there power in that palm. It hurt like you couldn't believe. From what I heard, Wesley got even worse from his dad. The whole thing felt so crazy that I thought the world was falling apart. So now, although being out of line was my favored mode of operation, there were just some things I didn't do. Like hang out in Old Town.

I never thought to question why it upset my father so much. I never thought to question a lot of things.

When I glanced up at Paula, she was looking down the sharp bulge in my shirt. The glove was out of sight, but definitely not out of mind for either of us.

"You didn't get it at a store, did you?" Paula said. She wasn't asking a question. She was stating a fact.

"I guess it's not exactly something you'll find at Wal-Mart," I answered.

I thought she was going to keep asking questions, but this time she chose not to — the same way I chose not to ask where Grant had gotten it from. That path of questioning led to a place I didn't want to go. Much better to stay grounded in things that were easy to explain. Like Old Town.

Up ahead was a house that was once painted green, but little of the paint remained. A broken swing adorned the porch, which overlooked a dead willow in the front yard. The door was swung open wide.

"Wanna check it out?" asked Paula.

No, I didn't. "Sure," I said.

The house had only been like this for twenty years, but as we stepped inside, it seemed to me that it could have been this way for a hundred. Peeling wallpaper, fallen shelves, a moldering sofa, and a busted TV still plugged in to a dead outlet. The floor was littered with broken glass and abandoned knickknacks. We stepped carefully, exploring with the care of archaeologists.

"The people who lived here probably just moved to another part of town," I offered.

"Or they died," Paula replied. "Live people usually don't leave this much stuff behind.

I nodded and casually glanced back at the front door, just to make sure it was still open. Something about being in Old Town made me feel much younger than almost-fifteen. I didn't like the feeling.

I was the one who noticed the message.

Paula had opened the pantry door to reveal age-old baking soda and a rat-gnawed box of cornflakes, when I caught the writing on the back of the door and swung it open wider.

It wasn't just writing — it was gouged into the wood, scratched as if someone had used one of the many kitchen utensils scattered on the floor to leave the message.

GOD HELP US

Paula shuddered.

"Dying people do weird things," I offered. "They could have been delirious — drunk — or maybe it was written by a bum — I'll bet this place gets full of them in the winter. . . ." I kept on talking and talking, making excuses and explanations, warning off that undeniable feeling that the people who died here might not have died from the flu. What a miserable time to discover my intuition.

Paula turned to look at me, and it seemed to me that she grew pale.

"Jason . . . ," she said. I didn't like the tone of her voice. It lacked her usual confidence. "You want to be spooked, Jason?"

I didn't think it was possible to be any more spooked than I already was. "Sure," I said.

"Then turn around."

Then I realized that she wasn't looking at me — she was looking past me. I didn't make a move at first, not daring to consider what she might be seeing, but I couldn't stand like that forever. I turned slowly, trying to prepare myself for whatever horror was behind me . . . but there was nothing there — just the empty, dirty kitchen.

And a crooked picture hanging on the wall.

It was your generic sort of school picture that had graced the family home since the invention of the camera. Unremarkable, except for the face.

The hair was longer and wilder, and the clothes were a

hideous mix of colors that clashed like a traffic accident in polyester. But the face —

"My God," I said, "it's Billy Chambers."

It wasn't his father; it wasn't a cousin — it was *him*. There was no denying that ugly mug.

I reached over and pulled the picture from its broken frame. Flipping it over, I found a faded date written on the back. June 1976. Years before any of us were even born.

"But Billy's *our* age," I said. "This can't be right." Apparently there was more to Billy Chambers than a horsey face and a pitching arm.

Paula took my hand. Not in a boyfriend-girlfriend sort of way, but in the way you have to when two suddenly feels safer than one.

"Jason," she said with a forced calm to her voice, "are there any BB's left in that glove of yours?"

"Yeah," I said.

"Then put it on, and let's get out of here."

4

Shot Night

I woke up the next morning with more energy than I usually have — as if the weirdnesses of the weekend had pumped me full of a high-grade fuel you can't normally find in Billington. I was in high spirits, in spite of the gloomy specter of my shots, which I'd have to take that afternoon.

If I had been spooked the day before, that feeling had now resolved into a charge of excitement. A weapon of exotic design, a desperate message carved on a pantry door, a picture that couldn't possibly be what it appeared — and all this from a town that had always been about as interesting as a test pattern.

At the time, I felt sure that the answers wouldn't be half as good as the questions, so I was in no great hurry to figure them out.

I sat with Wesley during lunch that day, eating cafeteria hamburgers that tasted like fried carpet lint, and talked about my eventful weekend. Well, I didn't really talk — I taunted. I wasn't about to go telling any of it to Wesley, since Wesley was known to broadcast his short-term memory over a wide band of frequencies. In fact, Wesley often promised to give away secrets he had not yet received, leaving him in a permanent state of gossip debt.

Still, he was my best friend, so I felt obliged to tell him something, even if that something turned out to be nothing.

"Yesterday me and somebody who shall remain nameless found some weird things in a location I can't divulge," I debriefed him. "Oh, and on Saturday somebody gave me something incredible that I shouldn't discuss."

Wesley considered this over a big bite of his lint-burger. Then he said, "Do you want your pickle?"

The whole episode could have ended there, if Paula hadn't come over to sit next to me.

"I'm going to check back-issues of the *Billington Bugle* this afternoon, to find out about that epidemic," she announced. "And then I'm going to try and find out who owned that house. You want to come?"

Wesley smirked. "Is this the somebody-who-shall-remain-nameless?"

Paula glanced at his grinning face, then turned to me. "Did I miss something?"

"I can't go with you," I told her, effectively sidestepping Wesley's proud moment of discovery. "I have to get my . . . you-know-whats today," I told her, pointing to my upper right arm.

She looked at me, not catching my meaning. "Excuse me?"

I began to shift uncomfortably. This wasn't exactly something one talked about in the school cafeteria. "You know . . . ," I whispered. "I have to go get my . . . monthlies."

"Monthly whats?" she said, way too loud. Wesley did that

leaning-away-like-he-didn't-know-us thing. I sighed, wondering if she were trying to embarrass me or just trying to show me that it was silly to feel embarrassed about it. The fact was, the monthly trip to the doctor was never something people mentioned aloud. It was a personal, private thing you didn't talk about. Anyway, that's the way I was raised.

"My shots," I finally said, turning beet red. "My monthly shots. There, I said it — are you happy?"

At the very mention of them, Wesley giggled like a little kid — but Paula just looked at me as if she were waiting for more.

"You mean allergy shots?" she said. Wesley snickered with his mouth closed, and pickle fragments flew out of his nose. She gave him that ten-foot-pole look that people often gave Wesley. "What's so funny?"

I was a microsecond away from saying, "Never mind," and forcing myself to forget this particular circus of pain — but then it occurred to me, however improbable it might sound, that she didn't know.

"You get them, too, right?" I asked.

"No," she answered.

Hearing that sobered Wesley up. "Oh, give me a break," he said. "Everybody gets them. . . . Don't they?"

I looked at both of them, and my brain began to get that eggbeater feeling again. "You mean you really don't get them?"

Paula shrugged. "Sorry."

"Is it a religious thing?" asked Wesley. "That you can't have shots?"

She gave him that ten-foot-pole look again.

There was an uncomfortable silence then. And for the first time I began to feel that the gap between us was far more profound than the distance between here and New Jersey.

The bell rang, and she got up. "I'll see you in class," she said. But our eyes didn't meet for the rest of the day.

That afternoon, my brain-beater feeling evolved into something new. I felt this giddy sense of being off-balance — not physically, but emotionally, as if my mental center of gravity was no longer inside me, but was somewhere off to the side. It was like being on a carnival tilt-a-whirl — I didn't know whether to yell for joy, or to throw up.

And later, as I felt Doc Fuller inject the stinging pink solution into the flesh of my arm, I found myself, oddly enough, thinking of Copernicus and wondering if he got that tilt-a-whirl feeling when he plotted the movement of the earth and discovered that the center of the universe was anywhere but here.

That night after my shots, I stayed in my room, shivering under my covers, as I listened to the wind wailing outside.

Dad stayed in his room, too, door closed, riding out the fever from his shots in a private, personal way. Mom, wisely, always scheduled her shots on a different day from Dad and I.

She came into my room somewhere between my chills and hot flashes. "Hungry?" she asked. She sat on my bed, handing me a bowl of homemade vanilla ice cream. It was a family tradition on shot night.

As I slowly let its sweet blandness soothe my swollen throat, I watched her busy herself tidying up the pigsty of my room.

Shot night was the only time she picked up after me, and, I have to admit, I took advantage of it by neglecting my room for several days before.

Maybe I was just half delirious, but there was something I noticed as I watched her clean up. She was meticulous — but it went beyond mere neatness. She didn't just toss my clothes into the hamper — she would feel their texture. She wouldn't just close the window — she would first take a deep breath, smelling the aroma of the trees. She wouldn't just shut my closet door — she would listen to the creaking sound it made.

As I thought about it, I realized that my father was much the same way. It had to do with the way he felt the wood that he carved. The way he savored even the most unimpressive of home-cooked meals. The way he enjoyed TV — from a football game to the most horrifically bad sitcom. They both lived their lives as if every moment, no matter how trivial, was a privilege. They derived such joy from just being.

How very sad it must be, I thought, to be so absorbed by the commonplace.

I wasn't like that. My tastes — my needs — stretched far beyond vanilla ice cream and a clean room.

Before my mom left the room, I dared to tell her something that had been rattling around in my head for most of the day.

"I'm worried about this girl in school," I said. "She says she doesn't get shots."

Mom didn't miss a beat — although I noticed she folded the same shirt twice. "Really," she said. "That's unusual."

"Is it?" I sat up in bed, feeling my bones creak. "Do you think there are other kids in school who don't get them?"

34

Mom, a whiz when it came to non-answers, bounced skill-fully over the question. "Their business is their business," she said. Her answer did tell me something. It told me that the shots weren't mandatory, that they weren't just another part of everyone's life as I was always led to assume. Maybe there were lots of kids at school who didn't get them.

"What do the shots do?" I asked. "What do they keep us from getting?"

She reached down and took the empty ice cream bowl from my hands.

"Appendicitis," she said, then left me alone to wrestle with her answer.

By the next day, Paula, had already discovered that (a) the town library had no information on what happened twenty years ago, (b) the *Billington Bugle* was missing several key months out of its own archives, and (c) it would take a psychic and a team of bloodhounds sniffing through paperwork to uncover the owners of those decaying homes in Old Town.

Paula and I spent our lunch alone in the computer lab, which could have fulfilled a certain dream of mine, except we actually *used* the computer.

In spite of its relative obscurity, Billington did in fact have its own on-ramp to the information superhighway. Aside from the satellite dishes, there were personal computers in most homes, and our school had full Internet access for anyone with a skill for navigation. It was one of those cruelties of the town — pro-viding us with all the information we'd ever need about places we'd probably never see.

That day, however, we discovered that the information

system in Billington was not designed for finding things *in-side* the town. With the world at our fingertips, finding anything about Billington was like trying to scratch your own back.

"What's taking so long?" Paula asked impatiently. I was running us through a haystack of databases, in search of electronic needles.

"It's cross-referencing about a zillion different things," I told her. "Give it a second or two."

Clearly this whole business was frustrating Paula, but where she felt frustration, I felt anticipation. It was like opening a present to find another gift-wrapped box inside.

The screen went blank, and the database spit out a pathetically small list of possibilities.

"That's it?" said Paula.

I had gone fishing for Billington flu epidemics in the National Health Institute's database, but the closest it came was finding an outbreak of measles in Biloxi.

"Well, if it happened, word didn't spread out of this town," I offered.

"It wasn't exactly the dark ages," snapped Paula. "There would have been doctors sent out — experts. There would be blood tests and all sorts of medical records."

I shrugged. "Apparently not."

The possibility of some sort of cover-up in Billington really tickled me. I tried to imagine Mom, Dad, and their goofy circle of friends in some absurd conspiracy. Ha! They couldn't conspire up a surprise party.

I suppose my grin didn't mesh with Paula's frustration, because she rapped me lightly on the arm. Problem was, she hit the wrong arm. A pulse of pain shot from my shoulder to fingertips, reminding me of my shot the day before. My fever, of course, had gone. It was gone when I woke up that morning, replaced by the heightened sense of well-being that always followed the injection. Mom had served waffles, and Dad had announced the thrilling highlights from the morning paper. It was as if it had never happened. It was always that way the morning after the shots. It was, in its own way, a conspiracy of silence that I was a part of.

"Sorry," Paula said, when she realized what she had done. Then she asked, "Do you think your shots have anything to do with that epidemic?"

I had considered the possibility. "Maybe," I said. But I was beginning to suspect that the connection could not be like anything we were considering, because that implied that the epidemic was really an epidemic and the shot was merely a vaccination. No one needed a vaccination every month.

"We could come back here after school," Paula suggested when the bell rang. "Search more databases until we find something."

I would have been happy to surf the Internet with her, but it was Tuesday.

I had seen Grant in the hall earlier. He had nodded a greeting, and although he didn't say it, the nod was a reminder to be there. At the barn. Today.

"I-I can't," I stammered.

Paula crossed her arms and tilted back in her chair. "More shots?" she said.

"Just a meeting. . . ."

"What kind of meeting?"

I realized that I was on the verge of becoming a new subject of investigation — until Wesley, who had been eavesdropping from the doorway, stepped in for the rescue.

"Boy Scouts," he said. "We're Boy Scouts."

Paula looked at me, amused. "You're a Boy Scout?"

I looked away, mortified by the mere suggestion, and I guess she took my embarrassment as an admission of guilt.

"A Boy Scout, huh?" she said. "Well, I guess everyone needs a deep, dark secret."

Then she sauntered out to class, still chuckling to herself.

Once she was gone, I turned to Wesley, fuming. "I didn't need your boneheaded help," I told him.

"Well, what were you going to tell her?" he asked. "I'll bet you've already told her too much already!"

It took me a second to realize what Wesley was saying. Then my jaw slipped open in dumb bewilderment — an expression I would soon be very familiar with.

Wesley grinned, intensely pleased to have me, for once, at a major disadvantage.

"See you in Old Town," he said as he left. "Don't forget your glove."

5

Target Practice

"Make your weapon an extension of your fighting spirit."

Behind a barn, beyond a hill, in the loneliest corner of Old Town Billington, I met thirty others that afternoon. I knew them all. Both boys and girls — some from my grade, some younger, but all familiar faces. Each wore an identical glove, fit to match the size of his or her arm.

"Feel your weapon's power become your own."

I had walked through the eerie streets of the ghost town alone, but as I had neared the barn, I saw them all sifting through the woods. They greeted me, as friends do, but there was suddenly a camaraderie that had never been there before. Like a secret club — no, like a secret *order*. A gathering of an elite few. A gathering with some deep significance I had yet to know.

"Who you are — who you think you are — leave it behind."

I stood beside Wesley in a huge clearing behind the barn. We were arranged in a circle, facing outward, carefully aiming at scarecrow targets in the distance. A rifle range with no rifles — only our ironclad wrists.

"Grant gave me my glove two months ago," Wesley told me over the constant sound of firing weapons. "I still need lots of practice, though."

My head was still spinning from the depth of his deception. I didn't know whether to be impressed by it or to punch him out. "Since when can *you* keep secrets?" I asked.

Wesley shrugged. "I can keep them when they're about me."

He pointed two fingers at two different targets and fired. There were some kids who had progressed to firing four-finger shots at a time, but as it was my first day, Grant had instructed me to focus on one finger at a time, until I could isolate my muscles and fire each one in succession, accurately hitting my target every time. As I had been practicing on my own, I mastered the exercise pretty quickly. It really annoyed Wes, whose eye-hand coordination never got beyond cutting his own meat.

"Your heads are filled with poison notions that are all untrue."

Grant paced the inner circumference of the circle, spouting encouragement and strange profundities behind us. His voice had the conviction of a prophet — quite different from his security-janitorial utterings around school. Even if I didn't know what he was talking about, it sounded important. It made me *feel* important. It made me feel part of something unusual and spectacular.

40

"Your destiny has been buried beneath a lifetime of lies."

I dared to fire in two directions at once. Both shots hit their targets.

"Claim your destiny."

Wesley grunted, as though chalking it up to beginner's luck, refusing to admit that I had already gotten better at it than him. I fired again, really beginning to enjoy the recoil as the bearings pulsed out of my fingertips.

"So what's the deal with Grant?" I asked when Grant's inner orbit had taken him to the far side of the circle.

Wes glanced at him and said, "His satellite dish is pointed in the wrong direction."

I laughed. "He's got a screw loose, you mean?"

Wesley just stared at me, blinking. "No, his satellite dish is pointed in the wrong direction. Next time you pass his house, check it out."

"Remember what you once were. Imagine what you'll soon become."

I turned to my target and fired again, but my concentration was gone. "So he's got some weird up-link going on? Maybe he's a spy," I suggested.

"Nah," said Wesley. "I think it's a government thing — and maybe we're guinea pigs testing out this new weapon." He fired two shots, and finally hit his targets. "Everyone's got a theory, but no one knows for sure."

Coming from a guy who had two months to consider what

might really be going on, Wesley's theory didn't ring true. But then I had a bit more information than he did. I thought of the picture of Billy Chambers, who was now standing ten feet away, chewing a wad of bubble gum as he aimed at his targets, as if it were just another baseball game. I thought of the message carved in the house down the street. I thought of Ethan, whose name was quickly slipping out of conversations. Out of sight and out of mind. Then I thought about Paula, and how she didn't get shots. Was it all related — or did I just *want* it to be?

"Your lives are about to become more important than any on earth. Be ready."

I cleared my throat and whispered to Wes, "Wes, I've been thinking, what if lots of people don't get shots?"

He giggled nervously at the mention of the word. "Yeah, and I'll bet they don't go to the bathroom, either — they just hold it in, like on TV."

"I'm serious!" I grabbed his arm, and he accidentally fired a shot into the grass, just missing my toe.

"Watch it!" he shouted.

"Wes, what if we're the only ones — only us kids here, and our parents?"

"You're being dumb," said Wes, but he didn't seem too sure of it.

I scanned the line of kids again. It wasn't just that all the faces were familiar — the *collection* of faces was familiar. I'd seen all of these kids together before.

When I finally realized where, I couldn't believe that I hadn't known from the beginning.

"We all go to the same church!" I announced to Wesley. On the occasions that my parents drag me to Holy Circle Nondenominational, these are the faces I see there. The ones I used to see in Sunday school. Maybe they weren't all friends of mine, but we were bound by that link.

"Your parents have chosen to forget. You'll make them remember."

Wes looked around him, like the connection between all of us was just a minor curiosity. "Yeah, I guess so," he said. "What's the big deal? I mean, there's only like four churches in Billington."

"Our parents all knew each other before we were born," I explained to Wesley. "These are the kids of our parents' closest friends."

I could see the machinery grinding in Wes's head, like an old-fashioned cash register, struggling to make change. Then finally *ka-ching!*

"Hey, that *is* kind of weird, huh?"

"Weird isn't the word." I knew that this wasn't just a realization — it was a major discovery. It was like stumbling over a hill to find yourself staring at the Grand Canyon. Too wide to take in its scope, too deep to fathom its depth.

"You think, maybe," said Wes, taking a good long look at his glove, "that the government's gone and done something to all of us?"

I shook my head. "I don't think the government's that organized." And then I added, "I don't think *any* government is."

"What, then?"

But my answer was a stutter, then silence. Too wide. Too deep. I was riding the tilt-a-whirl again.

Then I felt a firm hand on my shoulder. I knew it was Grant.

"You're a natural," he told me. "I knew you would be. There's no substitute for instinct." He looked at me like a proud father, and I have to admit that in the midst of everything I was feeling, I did feel proud. Proud enough to put questions to him that no one else had the nerve to ask.

"Why are we learning this? Why us? Why here in Old Town? And who *are* you?"

I could almost see the questions slide off the Teflon coat of his personality. He smiled, and tapped my shoulder again. "The question is not who am I, Jason, but who are you?"

In usual circumstances, enigmatic people piss me off. I guess because most people who try to be mysterious usually have nothing worth being mysterious about. But Grant was different. He did seem to have something he was keeping padlocked in his brain, and it gave him an aura of confidence that made my questions seem silly, and unimportant. I wanted to be annoyed, but instead I found myself admiring him. For as long as I've known him, I'd seen him as a janitor and little more. But now I'd never see him like that again.

Then he leaned over and whispered something to me.

"You can't imagine how different things will be tomorrow."

6

Man on First

I've never seen the ocean, but I know what it's like to ride the crest of a wave and feel part of something much larger than yourself.

When I left Old Town, I was feeling invincible. I knew there was still a mother lode of unanswered questions, but I wasn't afraid of them. At least not then. It had been a bright afternoon, filled with high spirits. Even Old Town didn't seem so eerie to me as I left.

The sunset was spectacular as I came out of the woods and into the open fields. The sky was orange, and the clouds flamed red and purple. Crosswinds sliced them into jagged, bold angles, and it seemed that the heavens were so intense that they overwhelmed the dreary earth below. The sky was mystical and larger than life.

But it wasn't just the sky. The immensity of what was brewing in Billington was something you could feel — something you could almost smell, like the ionized air after a thunderstorm.

I felt sure going home would catapult me back to the ordinary. Tuesday night was meat loaf and mashed potatoes night, followed by an evening of "quality time," which could be anything from renting a family movie to a game of Trivial Pursuit — which, in Billington, wasn't a game but a lifestyle choice.

No, I was meant for greater things on this wildly charged evening.

When I got to the road, I pulled my bike out from behind the tree where I had left it, and headed toward Paula's house.

"What are you doing here?"

"Whatever happened to *hello?*"

"Hello. What are you doing here?"

Paula was out front, throwing a Frisbee with her dog in the fading light. The dog growled, sniffed me, then returned its full attention to the Frisbee.

"I was just passing by," I said. "I guess I wanted to see if you found out anything new."

"Nothing," she said. "Except that people around here become borderline psychotic when you mention Old Town."

"Like how?"

"Like they suddenly have to go answer a phone I don't hear ringing or they look around anxiously as if someone had put them under surveillance."

"People are superstitious about it," I offered.

"Some," she agreed, "but for others, it seems to go beyond that."

The dog came back. I put down my pack, which held the heavy weight of my glove, then took the Frisbee and hurled it as far as I could.

When I turned back to Paula, I couldn't think of anything

worth saying, so I just smiled and kept looking at her. Under normal circumstances, an uncomfortable pause with a girl would have left me borderline psychotic myself — looking away, picking at my nails, grinding my teeth nervously — but not in this particular here and now. My aura of confidence was still lingering all around me.

"Why did you really come here?" she asked with a smirk.

I didn't answer. I just leaned forward and kissed her.

You should keep in mind that I was not a master of smooth moves — in fact, my general behavior around girls was the social equivalent of a midair collision. But this move was a perfect landing.

The dog returned and began to growl tentatively. Usually I like dogs.

Paula took the Frisbee and hurled it with her pitching arm. "Get lost, Mookie." I could tell she wanted both dog and disc to go as far as the next county.

The Frisbee went far but curved wildly and landed on her roof. Mookie went after it, oblivious.

I smiled. "Did I ruin your no-hitter?"

She punched me in the stomach, not hard enough to hurt.

"Don't even think of stealing second," she told me, "because I'll pick you off with no mercy."

And that was fine. I wasn't thinking any lofty goals here. That wasn't my style. Then it occurred to me that I really didn't have a style until that moment. I giggled, then kissed her again.

A few moments later, a screen door squeaked open and she pushed me away. Mrs. Quinn appeared, silhouetted against the door frame. I didn't know if she had seen, but I realized that

I didn't care. At that moment, I felt I could have charmed my way out of anything.

"Paula, come in for dinner," said her mom. "Who's that you're with?"

"Just a friend from school," she said. "We were talking about science."

Then Mrs. Quinn, who was not blessed with good night-vision, said, "Would she like to stay for dinner?"

"No," said Paula, "she was just leaving."

Mrs. Quinn went back inside, and Paula turned to me, but this time we both kept our distance.

You can't imagine how different things will be tomorrow, I thought, and smiled. I thought of the glove in my bag, and the unexpected boldness that had brought me to this moment. "Do you ever feel," I asked Paula, "like you're hanging on the edge of the biggest moment of your life?"

She rolled her eyes. "It's not that big a deal," she said. But then she realized that I wasn't just talking about us.

"What's going on with you, Jason?"

"I'll tell you the second I know," I promised her. I went over to her and kissed her again — just a quick one, like a pinch to make sure it was all real.

"See you in school," I said, and rode off boldly into the fading sunset.

When I got home, all was not well.

"I came to pick you up at school this afternoon, but you had already left," said Mom, with an urgency in her voice that had nothing to do with my lateness for dinner. In fact, I noticed there was no smell of meat loaf in the house at all. The table

48

was void of either utensils or leftovers. There was no dinner to-night, and she was busy going through drawers. "Where were you?" she asked.

"Just hanging out with Wesley," I told her, which wasn't entirely untrue.

She didn't seem concerned with my answer at all. I watched as she pulled some photos of the three of us from a drawer, then crossed to the sofa and slid them into the side of a suitcase. Suddenly my appetite, which had seemed all-important just a moment before, vanished. There was some powerful unpleas-antness going on. I swallowed hard, and my voice cracked as I asked, "Who's leaving?"

The door had opened, and Dad came in with another dusty suitcase he had pulled from the garage. "All of us," he said.

As I glanced into the bedroom, I saw more overstuffed suit-cases piled on the bed. I didn't even know we had that many suitcases — we never go anywhere.

"There's a case on your bed," said Mom. "I've already packed most of your clothes. Anything else you want, pack it in there."

"Where are we going?"

"Elsewhere," Dad answered. "Someplace far from here."

The moment had all the elements of a pillow-shredding nightmare: You finally start dating the girl of your dreams, and your parents decide it's time to enter the Witness Protection Program.

About a million thoughts, images, and emotions flashed through my mind. I thought I might yell at them; I thought I might demand some answers. I thought I might just take off

49

and run. But in the end, I realized that I had my own variable to add into this nasty little equation.

Instead of saying anything, I merely reached into my backpack and pulled out my glove, holding it in front of me, so that they could see.

It stopped them dead in their tracks. Considering the things Grant had been saying, I thought it might play a part in whatever was going on, but I never expected the reaction I got. They stared at me standing there defiantly. Finally Dad spoke, his face turning red.

"Where did you get that?" His voice was a furious growl.

I felt my hands shaking a bit but didn't give in to fear.

"First you tell me why we're packing."

In an instant Dad was on me. He grabbed me by my shirt and pushed me hard against the wall. I could hear things falling in the china cabinet on the other side.

"Who gave it to you?"

"John!" warned my mother.

My father loosened his grip. "Answer me!"

"The school janitor," I barked at him. "His name is Grant."

"I know who he is!" Dad shouted. Then he ripped the thing from my arms and flung it across the room. It hit the coffee table, bounced against the wall, and spilled its load of ball bearings all over the floor.

"You are to go to the garage, and you are to destroy it — do you understand me?"

"Not until you tell me *why*."

I thought he would hit me then. I actually thought he would haul off and belt me until I couldn't ask any more questions, but even in his feral parental state, he couldn't bring himself to do it. He backed off, and the phone began to ring.

Mom thought to let the machine get it but on the third ring, picked it up.

"Hello."

I heard a faint voice on the other end but only for a moment. She hung up quickly and loudly, then turned to Dad. "It was Grant," she said.

The little vomit-ride in my head started to spin in the other direction.

"Speak of the devil," I said.

My father ignored me. "What did he say?"

"He said if you don't call a meeting right now, he'll do it himself."

"Fine," snapped my father. "Let him call his own meeting." He zipped open the suitcase he had just brought in and continued packing, as if the issue was closed.

I put my fingers in my mouth and let loose an earsplitting whistle. "Hey! If you don't tell me what's going on here," I threatened, "I'll — I'll do something worse than anything I've ever done before!" Although for the life of me, I didn't know what that could possibly be.

Dad looked at me, in the way fathers do when they can't translate a generation down.

"You say Grant gave you the glove," he said. "What do you know about Grant?"

I shrugged. To be honest, there was only one thing I knew about Grant. "His satellite dish points in the wrong direction," I said.

The significance of that, which was lost on me, hit my father like a shock wave. He paced, and dragged his fingers nervously through his graying hair. "What has he told you? Has he said anything to you that sounded unusual?"

"Everything he says sounds unusual," I told them, realizing that I was giving information but still not getting any in return. "He said that you've forgotten, and it's up to us to remind you."

"Us?"

"There's about two dozen of us," I told him. "The kids from our church." And then I added, "They've all got gloves like mine."

Whatever wind was filling my parents' sails seemed to die when I told them that. Dad stalked away and got himself a beer from the refrigerator.

"We'll finish packing," he announced. "Then we'll call some of the others to let them know we're leaving. If they want to follow, it will be up to them."

I felt like screaming, but I knew that wouldn't get me anything. So instead, I searched out a rational, sensible corner of my mind and said, very calmly, "Mom, Dad, listen, I know that you're trying to protect me, but you can't. I'm not five years old, and I wish you'd respect me enough to tell me the truth."

They looked at each other, cornered by my sudden display of maturity and reason.

Dad turned to me, opened his mouth to say something, but closed it again. It was Mom who broke the silence.

"We're not . . . *from* here, Jason," she said.

Dad drew a deep breath and tried awfully hard not to look at me.

"What do you mean 'not from here'?" I sputtered. "You grew

up here — I've seen pictures of you as kids — Grandma and Grandpa are buried in the town graveyard!"

"Yes and no," my father said.

Yes and no. Okay, I thought. This is fine. My life hasn't necessarily been a lie; it's just been a huge half-truth. "So where are we from?" I asked. "Another state? Another country?"

Dad put down his empty beer bottle. "Think bigger, son."

I saw tears building in his eyes. I turned to my mother, and she couldn't even look me in the face. She turned and pulled the suitcase off the sofa, but she had never zipped it closed, and its contents clattered onto the floor — it was full of little glass vials, each filled with a thick pink liquid.

A lifetime's worth of our monthly shots.

I nodded. Okay, I said to myself. Okay. All right. I can deal with this. But the truth was, I couldn't. Instead, I let all of this information pile in my head like a stack of dirty clothes that would eventually need a washer, and I sat there in silence, watching Mom carefully pick up the vials.

I don't think Mom and Dad said a word to each other for the rest of that night. I don't even think they finished packing. By ten Mom had dropped into a restless sleep on the sofa, and then about an hour later I saw my father walking into the backyard alone. I slipped out the back door and followed.

It was a clear night, and the moon was high. Following him was easy. He held something in his hand, but it was a long time till I got a good look at what it was. When my eyes had fully adjusted to the light, I could tell that it was a handgun.

He walked a steady pace from one field to another, to another, until I could see where he was going. Our little church

53

was on the hill up ahead. The lights were on in there, and the lot was full of cars. I didn't even know he owned a gun.

He walked up the hill, striding toward the church, and I started to get more scared than I ever remembered being. I was about to call out to him — to let him know that I was there, and maybe that would shatter whatever plan he had — but he stopped halfway up the hill and just stared at the building.

I could hear voices inside — angry voices, troubled voices — but the voice coming from the pulpit was not Pastor Bob's. It was Grant's.

My father stood there a good ten minutes, then he made a course change, down off the hill, and toward the woods.

I followed him on to Old Town.

7

The Warrior-Fools

Like so many things in Billington, the Old Town storm cellar, where Paula had almost dropped my glove, turned out to be more than it appeared.

My father disappeared down the cellar, and I followed far behind. At the bottom of the steps, a false wall opened up to reveal a metal hatch on heavy hinges, and beyond the open hatch was a narrow, curving corridor. I ventured forward into a dim light that seemed to have no source.

It was a tight, self-contained place, like a submarine. Everything was a gunmetal gray, with valves and conduits winding around one another, down curved walls, and for an instant, I had the strangest impression that I was walking on the inside of my own glove. I shuddered.

Empty, dark chambers loomed on either side of me, but finally I came to one that was slightly brighter. It was a space not much larger than my bedroom, with dark walls and a rough steel floor. It was empty — it seemed that whatever had been in this place had been pulled out, scavenged for other purposes.

My father sat in there on a steel bench, looking forward at

nothing. He still held the revolver in his hand, with the safety off. I stepped into the room.

"Dad?"

He didn't seem surprised to see me. "I'm sorry I pushed you against the wall," he said, "but when I saw your training glove, I went a little crazy."

Training glove? I thought, but didn't dare to question him about it now.

I sat down on a bench across from him, not sure how to feel — I was still sort of piling up the laundry. I could tell what this place was but didn't dare ask about that, either. All I could do was watch my father's every move, every blink, and stare at the gun that rested in his lap.

He looked around. "Not much left of it, I'm afraid," he said. "We all agreed we'd dismantle as much as we could, then bury it. We couldn't do anything about the engines, but I doubt it will ever fly again."

"Dad, tell me who we are . . . who *I* am."

My father looked to me, then to the gun, then back to me, but still said nothing.

"I'll tell you what," I said to him. "Tell me the truth, and if it really sucks, you can give me the gun and I'll shoot you myself."

He laughed at that. I knew he would. Still, he kept the gun tightly in his grasp.

"I *have* told you, Jason," said my father. "I've told you hundreds of times."

But I just shook my head, not understanding.

"You would ask me to tell it every night," he continued. "Then one day you said you were too old to hear it anymore."

It came to me then in a flash of memory — something I

56

hadn't thought about for years. I gasped, and my gasp echoed in the lonely chamber. "The Warrior-Fools!"

My father nodded. "Do you still remember it?"

I searched my memory. Yes, I did remember! There are some things that you don't think of for years, but the second you do, they burst forth — every word, every image. That's how deeply it had been ingrained in my mind. That's how carefully my father had put it there. I could still hear my father's tone of voice as he told it. Always the same. He would tell it with passion and tenderness. It wasn't so much the story but the way he told it that made me want to hear it so many times, all those years ago. Now I tried to tell it back to him in the same way.

"Once upon a time," I began, "there sailed a ship of fools who fancied themselves warriors. . . ."

My father smiled. I continued: "They were strange of face and strong of mind, with powerful bodies and arms of fire. Monsters all, who believed themselves beautiful. On a voyage of conquest they sailed, but their arrogance grew into a tornado that cast them on the shores of the new land. Their shattered ship spilled poison that destroyed the good, fragile people of the land they would conquer." I looked up at my father incredulously. "Old Town?"

"It wasn't Old Town when we arrived," he said.

I closed my eyes, piecing together the rest of the story word by word. "With each rising of the sun, the Warrior-Fools stared at the horizon, waiting for the thousand ships they would lead into battle — but the ships didn't come, and the sunrises became too many to count. So they worked the land, lived the lives, and walked the ways of the fragile people, until their hearts filled with a joy and a peace they had never known as

Warriors and Fools. Then, one day, they rose from their labors and looked at themselves. The mirror no longer showed them the monsters that they had been, for now they had become the very people they destroyed, from the top of their heads to the bottom of their souls. And no one mourned that the Warrior-Fools were no more."

In the silence that followed, I went over the story again and again in my mind, finally knowing what it said. What it meant.

My father finally spoke.

"We came from a race of conquerors, sent to prepare for an invasion that never came," he explained. "We couldn't do anything for the people dying in Old Town. We had ruptured a fuel cell in the storm, and there was just too much radiation." He began to rub his eyes as he thought about it. "We took care of them, and took samples of their genetic structure. Some of the samples we saved; other samples we wrapped around our own, masking ourselves on a molecular level. As they lay dying, they watched as we became them. It must have been horrible for them."

As I listened, I tried to imagine it from both sides, but the two different points of view wouldn't mesh in mind.

"So . . . we're body snatchers?" I said, letting out a nauseated little chuckle.

"It's not that cut and dry," he said. "Their DNA was all we had to mask ourselves."

Then something occurred to me. The very thought of what I was about to ask made my mouth dry, and my voice hissed out in a jagged whisper: "Why did we need to mask ourselves?" I asked. "What do we look like?"

But he wouldn't answer that one.

He went on to tell me how the forty of them cleaned the crash site and buried the ship. How they hid the truth from the rest of the town, by becoming the humans who had died, down to every last detail of their lives. "We took over their jobs, their friendships, their habits, and beliefs," he told me. "We replaced them, and for the ones who died that we couldn't replace, we invented the epidemic. The act we put on was so convincing, the rest of Billington believed us."

He kept pouring forth his grand confession, and the more he spoke, the easier it flowed. Soon his voice had slipped into that tone of simple conversation that made everything he said sound reasonable, as if he were talking about last month's fishing trip.

"We moved out of Old Town a family at a time and just disappeared into other neighborhoods. It was easy after that."

It's funny, but in spite of how limited my own life experience had been, accepting the truth had become remarkably easy. My father could have told me that we were made of pipe cleaners and pie filling, and I would have nodded and asked him what flavor.

"We gathered information," he continued, "studying the strengths and weaknesses of humans from the inside out, looking for ways to exploit them. We became students of human nature. And then something happened that we never expected."

I thought back to the old bedtime story. "You liked it here?" I said in disbelief. The concept of actually *liking* Billington was way too far-fetched for me.

"Not just *here*," he said. "We liked everything. The change of the seasons, the taste of the food, the smell of the air. But most of all, we liked who we were and the way we lived." He took a look at the gun, then finally put it down and pushed it out of reach. "They never contacted us. No ships ever came. And we abandoned the mission when the first of us had a child. That was Ethan."

Hearing Ethan's name made my heart seize for a painful beat. I wanted to ask what he really died of but wasn't sure I was ready for the answer.

"Ethan was the first child born," said my father. "You were the second."

Neither of us spoke for a while, and in the silence, the numbness I felt settled deeper into my bones. I guess you would call it shock, but it wasn't what I'd expected shock to feel like. It felt more like being in a cocoon.

"There's something I need to show you," my father said — but I could tell by the way he said it that it wasn't something he wanted to show me. He *needed* to show me. It was something I suddenly had the right to know.

Reaching into his pocket, he pulled out a photograph and handed it to me. It was a Polaroid of a man in his mid-thirties. A pleasant but unremarkable-looking man. Thinning brown hair. Ordinary features. His smile seemed familiar.

"His name was J.J. Pohl," explained my father. "He was a town hero here. Fought in Vietnam, then took over his father's hardware store in Old Town." Again he rubbed his eyes from the sting of the memory. "Your mother and I took care of him as he lay dying, a few weeks after our arrival. We had already taken on the forms of the people we were to be. There were only forty of us, but more than seventy died — leaving more people than we could replace. J.J. was one of those.

"Just before he died, he made me promise him something: that no matter how many of us came, no matter how powerful our forces were, something human would be saved. I didn't know how I'd ever have the power to keep such a promise, but I promised him anyway. He was a good man, who didn't deserve the kind of death we had brought him."

Dad looked down, rubbing his feet across the dusty metal floor. "Anyway, we took a sample of his DNA before he died. And seven years later, we used it to wrap around the genes of our own son. We gave him to you."

It took a few moments for the significance of that to wind its way home. I looked to the picture again, and when I did, my hand shook. The smile was mine. The eyes were mine. This ordinary man with a forgettable face was me. I thought of the other kids who were part of this. Wesley, Billy Chambers, and more than twenty others. Was there an old picture of a dead townie who looked like Wes, just as there was one for Billy Chambers and for me? Is this all we were? To find out that your life is a lie is one thing, but to find out that your own face doesn't even belong to you —

I wanted to take my hands and gouge my face until it was gone, but it wasn't like peeling off a latex mask. This living disguise went down to the bone. Down to every single cell of my counterfeit body. The numbness I had felt was gone. Whatever weird mental cocoon had held me through these revelations now burst apart. I couldn't tell what was emerging from it.

I forced myself to look my father in the face.

"How could you do it? How could you give me this — this small-town nobody," I said, waving the picture at him, "when I came from *this*?" And I raised my hand to the ship around me.

"We chose to be human," he insisted. "And we never regret-ted the choice!"

"I had no choice," I shouted. "You made me live this lie!"

"We never gave you a lie," he said, his voice booming in the metal chamber. "We gave you a new truth. A *better* truth."

"A better truth, huh? Well, you know what you can do with your 'better truth.'" With that I stood and stormed toward the door. I didn't know where I would go, but I knew that I couldn't stay there with him, gun or not. Then he said something that stopped me in my tracks.

"The story's not over."

I turned back to him slowly. "What's that supposed to mean?"

"There's a new chapter to the Warrior-Fools."

He stood up, and although he was a big man, he seemed diminished in the dim light of the black steel room.

"Many years later," he began, "the last of the Warrior-Fools stared at the horizon, his satellite dish pointing in the wrong direction. And one day a message fell upon his ears: '*The thousand ships are on their way.*'"

Far away I could hear the wind breathing across the mouth of the storm cellar, and the cold chambers of the buried ship resonated with a lonely moan. It didn't take a brain surgeon to figure out who that last Warrior-Fool was. And why he had secretly given all the kids training gloves.

"When?" I asked.

My father shook his head. "The message was garbled," he said. "We know they're coming, but we don't know when. Grant has known about it for months but just told us today. I suppose he was waiting until he got his hands on every last kid."

And I must have been that last kid. My eyes began to sting — maybe from suddenly being opened so completely. I began to rub them, and realized that they weren't my eyes at all. They were J.J. Pohl's.

We climbed out of the dead ship, then up the moss-covered steps of the storm cellar, into the cool night. The trees swayed with the breeze, as they always did. The stars were the same, and yet it was hard to believe that this was the same world I had climbed down from just a short time ago. There were probably a million things to say to each other, but neither of us seemed to know what those things could be. Dad looked down at the gun he was holding, then flipped open the barrel and pulled out the bullets, one by one. Then he handed me the unloaded weapon.

"I want you to bring this home," he told me, "and tell your mother I've gone to the meeting. Tell her to meet me there."

"What are you going to do?"

My father, who always seemed to have a definite mind on everything, just looked at me and said, "I have no idea. What do you think I should do?"

It was the first time I could ever remember my father asking my advice on anything. I could sense the power I had in the moment.

"I think maybe you should do what Grant says," I told him. "I mean, wasn't he your Fearless Leader?"

But my father shook his head. "No, Jason," he said. "I was the leader."

And with that, he turned and left.

I stood there alone in the weed-choked darkness, gripping

the picture of J.J. Pohl in my hand. It was as if I had to teach myself to walk and breathe and think all over again. I looked down at the picture. In the darkness, I couldn't see the face anymore. Just as well.

This picture isn't me, I told myself. I might have his body, and his birthmarks, and his B.O., but it's not me, not anymore.

I slipped the picture into my pocket and began lifting my feet, one after another, until I was out of Old Town and on my way home. And with each step, my sense of resolve grew. I didn't know what my parents were going to do, but things were beginning to fall into place for me.

I now felt an electrified sense of purpose. The unimpressive, unimportant life I had led before had died — I felt no remorse about that. What lay ahead was a lifetime of unexplored terrain, and I was more than ready to explore it and to find out who and what I was.

8

Pigs in a Blanket

The sun burst upon a clear day that was just like any other, and yet like none other. Grant was right about that. When I woke up, I felt strange about the whole thing, like when you make an idiot of yourself at a party but don't realize it until after you get home.

My parents hadn't returned from the meeting. I imagined they would be gone for most of the day taking care of strange business. So I sat around alone, looking at J.J. Pohl's teenage reflection in the mirror. Then I paced around the house, trying to find something appropriate to do under the circumstances. What do you do the morning after you find out you're an extraterrestrial? I had some Wheaties, then went off to school.

I had been the last one to be brought into Grant's little legion of space cadets, but the first one to know the truth about who we were.

The others found out soon enough, though.

None of them were in school that day — apparently the other parents had all decided it was better to hear the truth from them, rather than from other kids. Kind of like sex education.

From the stories I heard, each kid took it differently. Wesley cried for six hours straight, then went out to get a burger. Roxanne sat in front of her vanity, spreading bizarre shades of makeup all over her face, trying to figure out what she might really look like. Billy Chambers went out to practice his pitching, figuring now he *really* had an edge over Paula. And everyone thought of Ethan. We all wondered what he would have said about it.

I stood at my locker, just beginning to realize that Wesley and the others were being given their dehumanization presentations by their parents that morning, so none of them were going to show. But Paula was there, and she was the only one that could momentarily take my mind away from the other events laying claim to my brain. She made a straight line to me through the crowded hallway. I had to smile. Other girls and guys, they play games with each other. They pretend they "just happen to be wandering by" when they suddenly notice each other, as if they hadn't planned the whole thing. Paula was above all that.

As she came closer, I noticed that her hair had a silky sheen to it, as if she had brushed it half a million times or so. She was wearing a baseball cap, so I had to look close to tell. Which I did.

"Hi," I said. "You look nice."

She smiled, seeming pleased that I was really looking. "Thanks. I wish I could say the same for you, though."

I glanced down at myself, to realize that I was an unqualified mess. I was still wearing the same pants and wrinkled shirt from the day before, and my tangled hair must have looked like it was harboring a fugitive tornado.

I sighed, too tired to feel the appropriate level of embarrassment. "I'm not really this gross," I explained. "There have just been some problems at home. My head was somewhere else, I guess."

She took off her baseball cap and slipped it on my head. "Here," she said tenderly. "You need it more than I do." Then she tossed me a smile and headed off to class.

It took me only an instant to realize what she had done. Most of the guys on teams, they give their girlfriends their caps or jerseys or whatever — but I wasn't on a sports team, which meant I didn't have anything to give Paula. So she had given her cap to me, and she'd done it in a way that was easy and didn't make either of us feel self-conscious about it. I didn't know if there were any other guys in school who dared to wear their girlfriend's accessories, but I, for one, was pretty pleased to have this particular Billington Bullet's cap on my head.

"Paula," I called to her before she went into her classroom. I wanted to tell her the whole thing. Everything I knew about myself. I wanted to share my amazement with her, and somehow make her a part of this, too. But with all the nerve I'd developed lately, I didn't have the nerve to tell her.

"Thanks, Paula," I said. "You're great."

On my way home, I spotted Wesley in Banzai Burger, sitting alone, scarfing a Triple-Patty Deluxe. That was the way Wes dealt with problems — he ate them alive, and for a guy so skinny, he could sure put it away. I went in and sat down next to him.

67

"You're gonna blimp out if you keep eating like that," I said, pointing at the ketchup-oozing burger clamped between his fingers. There were two empty wrappers already on the table.

"My parents always said I got a black hole in my stomach. Now I figure, they might have been telling the truth." He took a healthy bite, almost getting one of his fingers. He glanced up, clearly noticing Paula's cap on my head, but didn't say anything about it.

"How'd your parents tell you?" I asked him.

"We played twenty questions," he answered, then took another bite of his burger and spoke through a mouthful of food. "Y'know, Ralphy Sherman always said there were aliens in town."

I smirked. "Yeah, and Ralphy Sherman also says he was Elvis in a previous life. This time I think it was just a lucky guess."

Wesley swallowed such a huge bite that I could see his throat bulge, and then he forced up a shrug. "So, we're alien — so? What's the big deal?"

But it *was* a big deal. You could tell by the way he inhaled the rest of that hamburger. It got me thinking about that black-hole theory, too.

"Wes," I said, "this is a *good* thing."

He wiped the ketchup from his face and examined me, trying to see how sure I was. "You think so?"

"Of course it is. We've got something that no one else has. We're special. We're *better*."

Wes slurped his soda. "You know, your dad's in charge," he said. "My parents say he walked right into the church and took over. Grant just stepped down."

I was thrilled to hear it but tried not to overstate my enthusiasm. "So was Grant mad?"

Wesley shrugged. "He got put in charge of us, which is what he wanted, so I guess he's okay with it." He pushed his fourth burger at me. "Take it — I'll puke if I have another one."

Wesley watched me eat for a few moments, and then said, "The new weeklies sure won't be any fun."

I turned to him, wondering what he could possibly be talking about.

"What weeklies? Don't you mean monthlies?"

"Didn't you hear? Your father okayed it this morning."

I put down the burger. "I've been at school. Enlighten me."

Wesley looked around, to make sure no one else was eavesdropping, as if anyone would believe what they heard anyway. Then he leaned across the table and spoke in a strained whisper. "The shots we've been getting keep us looking like we do," he said, "but they weren't designed to be used on teenagers, on account of our bodies are changing and stuff. Anyway, that's why Ethan died. He kind of got allergic to being human."

It was the first hint I had gotten of what really happened to Ethan, but I didn't want Wes to know it hit me that hard. I swallowed, then pulled away Wes's Coke and took a big gulp, to keep down what I had just eaten.

"So?"

"So," said Wes, "they want to make sure it doesn't happen to us. They've changed the formula and broken it into four doses. Now we have to get treatments once a week instead of once a month."

I thought about it. "If my father said it was the right thing to do, then it probably is," I announced to Wes. Getting poked in the arm on a regular basis was not my idea of fun, but there were worse things. "I mean, this whole thing that's happened to us — when you think about it, it's kind of like winning the lottery. That's got to be worth a few extra trips to Doc Fuller's."

Wesley grinned slightly. "You got this thing figured out pretty good, don't you? I wish I could be like you."

I shrugged. "You are like me," I reminded him. Whatever that meant.

Explosive genetic dischelation. That's what happened to Ethan. It was a fancy way of saying that in addition to generating body odor and pubic hair, his adolescent body suddenly rejected his human genes. It was messy; it was painful — it was a hormonal thing. At least that's how my father explained it, again in that casual fishing-trip voice, as if we were talking about scaling trout. I realized that he was in his own state of shock and that it might last a good long time. Perhaps he had to live in shock to get through this.

It was dusk when Dad got home that night. He found me out in the garage alone, running my fingers along the half-finished cabinets in there. I had been there for ten minutes or so, feeling where the wood was rough and where it was smooth. Finding all the edges that were incomplete. When Dad opened the door, catching me, I turned red, as if I'd been caught doing something wrong.

"I thought you'd be off with Grant," he said.

I shrugged. "I thought you didn't like Grant."

He shook his head. "No room for that sort of thing anymore. Grant volunteered to teach you kids. To train you. He'll do a good job, so I gave him my blessing."

70

He stepped deeper into the garage and rubbed his own hands across his smooth, well-crafted furniture, then looked at his tool chest for a few moments. Then he slowly lowered the lid, as if he were closing a casket.

"I suppose it was time for all of us to stop playing," he said. Funny, because I always thought of what he did as work. I thought about the invasion and wondered who'd need hand-crafted furniture anymore once ships began dropping from the sky. The thought was so absurd, it made me laugh out loud.

Dad took a good look at me, as though he were looking for cracks.

"Where'd you get the cap?" he asked, and it occurred to me that I hadn't told him about Paula. Not that I would have told him under normal circumstances, but now it seemed I had more reasons to keep it to myself.

"I robbed the Little League coach at gunpoint," I told him with a shrug.

To which he responded, "Didn't I tell you to give that gun to your mother?"

We both grinned at each other's twisted sense of humor. I guess it relieved the tension enough for him not to care where I really got it.

We went to the kitchen and cooked up some frozen dinners — which had always been a criminal offense in Mom's book. Mom, however, had apparently changed her tune, because the only sign that she had even been home was a note on the table and a freezer full of Hearty-Man turkey and Salisbury steak.

"She's got a lot of work ahead of her," said Dad as we ate. I had already eaten one dinner but sat with him to eat another.

"Since we don't know how long we have, she has to prepare a strategy for the arrival."

"I never thought of Mom as being strategic," I said.

Dad laughed. "She had to be a master of strategy to deal with you."

I laughed as well, but there was something about the way he said that, that bothered me. After a few moments I realized what it was. He said it in the past tense. She *had* to be a master of strategy to deal with me. As if she wasn't going to be dealing with me anymore.

He explained to me all about Ethan's unpleasant end as he scooped up peas and stuffing — it's amazing the things you can talk about while eating. Then, when the meal was done, he looked up from his empty plastic tray. "Are you okay with all of this, son?" he asked. It was kind of a lame thing to ask, considering. I mean, if I wasn't okay with it, what difference would it have made?

"Are you kidding?" I told him. "It's an adventure; it's great."

He smiled. "Grant was right," he said. "You're going to do very well for yourself."

He left a few minutes later to return to his new duties as Fearless Leader. I didn't see him or Mom again for days.

"A strong, solid move."

"Thanks. My dad and I used to play a lot."

On the third day of my new life, Grant and I played chess in the little abandoned diner in Old Town. Around us were the other members of our little after-school club. The place had been filthy when we arrived, but Grant had set us to the task of cleaning up what we could. Twenty years of grime comes clean pretty quick when two dozen kids are working at it. At the time, I had thought we came to this place as a matter of convenience. We had been doing drills behind the barn with our training gloves, which was now a daily activity, when dark clouds began looming over the hills. Before the storm let loose, Grant had brought us here. By now I should have known that nothing he did was random.

"You've been anticipating my moves," said Grant, pensively stroking his beard. "How intuitive of you."

That one caught me by surprise. No one had ever accused me of having intuition. It distracted me enough to make a lousy move.

"I'm not intuitive, just observant," I told him.

"Even better," he said. "Being observant means knowing *why* your intuition tells you something." Then he leapt his knight over a row of pawns and captured my king's rook. "Of course, nobody's perfect," he added.

With the diner clean, the other kids busied themselves discussing form and style in the use of their gloves. A few tables over, Billy Chambers, who was a half-decent artist, drew pencil renderings of what we might really look like, but most of his sketches had lobster claws and fangs that were vicious enough to make the younger kids grow pale in mortal terror. So now he was depicting us as Smurfs, which wasn't too thrilling a thought, either. He kept bringing his drawings over to Grant, who would just look at them, chuckle, and say, "Keep trying," although he would never suggest what Billy ought to do differently.

Over at the table next to us, Wesley was talking to a few fifth graders, the youngest kids in the group, trying to explain genetic chelation to them, as if he had it all figured out.

"You know those little cocktail weenies?" Wesley was saying. "The ones with dough wrapped around them?"

"Pigs in a blanket," responded one of his astute pupils.

"Yeah, pigs in a blanket. Well, imagine that every cell in our body is a pig in a blanket. Billions and billions of them, all wrapped up like that. Well, we gotta make sure those pigs don't pop out of their blankets all at once —"

"Or else we'll just be a bunch of weenies," offered the astute pupil. Everyone but Wesley laughed.

"You're missing the point," he said, and tried using chocolate-covered peanuts as an analogy.

Without thinking about it, I reached over and touched my arm, where I had received my new and improved treatment the afternoon before. All the kids had gotten them, right here in Old Town. Smilin' Doc Fuller made a house call to an abandoned house Grant had brought us to. While we waited, Grant had suggested we clean the place up, just as we cleaned the diner today. The new treatment didn't make me feel sick, but I did feel something. My fingers and toes tingled all night. My back was itchy, and I could feel my neck hairs standing on end. I could feel those neck hairs now, but maybe that was just because I was here, face to face with Grant.

Lightning struck silently outside, and Grant captured my queen's knight. "You're losing focus on the game. What's on your mind?" Thunder pealed in the distance.

"You seem to know everything," I told him. "You tell me."

"It's not that I know everything," he said. "I'm just observant. Like you."

"So what do you observe about me?" I asked.

He fiddled with the knight he had taken as he looked at me and said, "You're good at a great many things, but you don't let on. You could get straight A's but you wouldn't give your teachers the satisfaction. The truth is, you have more brain power than you know what to do with."

I looked down to the chessboard and made a half-decent move. "Do you always have to talk like you're looking into a crystal ball?" I asked him.

He laughed. Lightning struck again, far away. "I call it as I see it." He waited a moment, as the thunder rolled deep and ominous.

By now, Wesley had leaned over from the other table, mesmerized, as if Grant were talking about him. More of the attention of the room had focused on our game and our conversation. That fact was not lost on Grant.

"I'll tell you a secret," he said to me, as the others leaned in closer to hear. "It's not just you — it's everyone here. All their lives, they've been better and brighter than the other kids in Billington, even if they've never known it. That's your starting point, and you'll only grow once the ships arrive."

"Why are they coming at all?" asked one kid. He was a sixth grader named Ford, but everyone called him Ferrari. "Why are we invading?"

Grant looked at him curiously, as if it should have been obvious. "Because we can," he said, and then added, "Because this world deserves better."

The kids around me sat a bit taller, as if trying to feel high and mighty.

"So what's going to happen to the others when the ships get here?" Ferrari asked.

Grant evaded that question like a stealth bomber evading radar. "Look around at your friends here," he instructed. "Fill your minds with them, and with your parents. As for everyone else, they're not your concern now. That will all work itself out."

And it was that simple.

Grant had a gift for making something true merely by speaking it. It was as if he had waved his hand and instantly, magically, freed us from responsibility. *The rest of the world was not our concern.* They were all people we had never seen, lives that never crossed our paths — and as for those people we did know, they would be forgotten. Replaced by the powerful vision of a new destiny.

It's incredible the things you'll let yourself think — the things you'll let yourself *do*, when the right person gives you permission.

Almost like a reflex, I reached up and adjusted my cap as I began to consider where Paula fit in to all of this. Well, if I was as smart as Grant said, then I'd find a way to make it work out. But for now I tried to put it as far out of my mind as I could. Focusing on the game, I slid my queen across the board in a brilliant, devastating move.

"Mr. Grant?" It was a girl's voice this time. I turned to see Amy, Ethan's kid sister, raising her hand. She was the youngest one Grant had brought into the group, having just turned ten. "Mr. Grant," she said, "when the others come, are they going to be horrible? Are they gonna look like monsters?"

Grant reached out his hand, beckoning her closer. He, like everyone else, had been particularly gentle with her since her brother died. She tentatively came forward.

"You don't have to worry about that, Amy," he said with

enough tender authority to quiet any fears the girl had. He reached out and touched her fine blond hair. "They're very beautiful."

"Beautiful to who?" I dared to ask. All the attention turned to me. "A snake is beautiful to another snake. A rat is beautiful to another rat."

He looked at me sharply and carefully weighed his answer.

"If a rat knew the difference, it would choose to be human. If a human knew the difference, it would choose to be one of us." He let his answer resonate through another peal of thunder, and then put me in checkmate in less than three moves.

9
Members Only

I don't know when I actually started thinking of myself as one of us instead of one of them — "us" being our little church group and "them" being everyone else. That kind of thinking grows inside you too slow to see, but too fast to stop — like the roots of a tree. I heard a story once about how a tree root burst through the metal side of a swimming pool, filling its water with cloudy mud. When something starts to grow deep, it grows strong.

It wasn't just Grant anymore, or our parents. In that first week, we had already started to cling together, looking out for each other — protecting each other. Isolating ourselves from the rest of town.

We are magnificent, Grant had said in his profound way. *We are above and beyond all others.* Deep down everyone wants to believe something like that, so going along with it felt like something natural, no matter how unnatural all the rest felt.

We visited the Old Town diner again the next day, and the day after that — it was quickly becoming an afternoon clubhouse for us in these last few days of the school year. And each afternoon, Grant fed us before he sent us off to our homes.

In just five days, home had come to mean an empty place, filled with an uncanny silence that remained even when I turned on my stereo and blasted the TV. The truth is, I no longer felt like myself. The dull routine that had ruled my life was gone — but there was only so much jumping for joy that I could do until that got boring, too.

Every evening I saw Paula. No matter how exhausted I felt, I would meet her at the mall or Banzai Burger or the batting cages — anyplace we could go to be together. We would talk about pointless things, and that was okay, since the important part was just talking. Every once in a while she would start bringing up that picture of Billy Chambers, or the message written in that house in Old Town, or my glove, which I should never have shown her. I would always find a smooth way of changing the subject, and she would let me. It was nice to know that she was more interested in me than in the mystery.

I wondered how much more interested she would be in me if she knew what I knew. Still, I couldn't tell her and refused to think about the day I would have to. Leading a double life isn't so hard to do when you live it day to day, pretending tomorrow will take care of itself.

On the last night of school, everyone turned out for a dance at the gym. Grant was there in his security guard capacity, keeping the peace and keeping an eye on me. I was the only one of us dancing with a girl from the outside. I was the only one of us dancing, period. The others all sat together like they were in their own glass bubble, talking and laughing as though the rest of the party didn't exist.

"Come sit with us," they had all urged me when I first arrived. They even had a seat at their table saved for me. I felt drawn to them and wanted to take my place there, but there wasn't a chair for Paula.

"Not much for dancing, are you?" Paula said during the second song. She sensed that my heart wasn't in it but misread the reason. Since we'd promised each other that we'd never become one of those pathetically clinging couples, I went out for some much-needed air while she gave some mercy dances to a few dateless guys on the sidelines.

Outside I found Wesley sitting alone on the steps, staring out like a depressive zombie. He held a glass of punch in his hand but didn't seem to be drinking it.

"Why don't you go dance?" I asked him.

"Nah, I got three left feet," he answered, which for all I knew could have been true.

"So I gave my mom my report card today, and she didn't even look at it, like it didn't even matter to her anymore. And I can't remember the last time I saw my dad. What do you think our parents do all day?"

I shrugged. "Wild parties," I told him. "They're guzzling margaritas and doing the limbo." I loosened my tie and took a deep breath. "I don't have a clue."

All of our parents were no doubt layered in deep secret meetings in the guise of barbecues and bridge parties. Whatever occupied their days and nights now completely mystified me, and it occurred to me that my parents had never mystified me before. There were lots of kids I knew whose parents had

80

office jobs. When you asked them about their parents' work, they would say things like "Oh, my dad's in distribution" or "My mom's a manager," but when you asked them what their parents actually did all day, no one really knew. At least with my parents, I could see the cause and effect of their labors. Mom busted her butt to keep our home and lives in working order, no matter how badly I sabotaged those efforts. Dad spun wood into cash, with the skill of his hands. It was all right there for me to see — but now that simplicity was gone. Thinking about it made my back itch and neck hairs stand on end again.

"Jason, can I ask you something?"

"Sure, go ahead."

Wes cleared his throat. "Do you think I'm smart?"

It was too serious a question to give a snide response. "You're okay," I said to him. "You get good grades. Yeah, you're smart."

"I do get good grades," he reminded himself, "and I could do better if I really wanted to."

I had to admit he was right. No matter what ridiculous things Wesley said or did, he did have that innate intelligence Grant was talking about. Common sense and wisdom seemed to be the real culprits in Wesley's case. He had about as much wisdom as a lampshade.

"So I'm smart, and you're smart — we're all smart," he said. "And Grant says we're better than everyone else. But the thing is . . . why don't I feel 'better'?"

I wanted to toss my hair back contemptuously and shrug off the question, but it was too big to dismiss with a shrug. I knew how he felt.

"We have to get used to being different," I suggested. "Then when we see what the differences are, maybe then we'll feel" — I felt the word crowding my brain, and I had to spit it out — "superior."

Wesley thought about it. I could almost see how the word was swelling in his brain, too. Like a big, thick root.

"You know, I do kind of feel that way when we're all together, like when we're doing target practice and even when we're just hanging out with Grant."

I nodded, and thought of the days and weeks ahead. "I think that we're all gonna be spending a lot more time together."

Wesley watched me closely, using me as a barometer for how he was supposed to feel. "And that's a good thing, right?"

I thought about that. Wesley and I were both only-children. To suddenly be in the company of what amounted to two dozen or so brothers and sisters didn't feel bad at all. It was the times alone when everything felt uncertain. The less time alone, the better.

"It's a very good thing," I told him, and making him believe it made me believe it even more.

The thing about collision courses is that if you could see them coming, you'd avoid the collision — but that would require having well-functioning radar, and my own personal radar dish was swinging back and forth so quickly, I wouldn't have noticed an ocean liner plowing down the driveway.

So naturally, when Paula came waltzing into the diner in Old Town, I was about as speechless as a mime in shackles.

It was a week after school had let out for the summer — about three weeks into my new life. The time had gone by so quickly, I could almost feel the whiplash. We were all getting used to the routine now. Our parents left at dawn and didn't come home until after we were asleep — sometimes they stayed at friends' homes rather than come home. Same on weekends. As for us, we would spend our nights sleeping over at each other's homes to keep from being alone with our thoughts.

During the days, Grant kept our hands and minds filled with glove training and with renovating Old Town. One of the parents even hooked up a generator while we weren't looking, giving the diner electricity.

Grant's training was both grueling and exhilarating, from marathon skill sessions with our gloves, to exotic mental exercises aimed at sharpening our minds to a lethal edge.

But on Thursday afternoon, a week after the end of school, we weren't quite practicing our skills. We were sitting in the diner, in two rows, scratching each other's backs.

It turns out the itching that had kept me awake that first night after our new treatment never quite went away, and it wasn't just me — so lately one of the joys of our afternoons had become our communal back scratch.

Since Paula had gotten herself a summer job at the community pool, I figured I wouldn't have to explain to her what I did with most of my days. But I guess she got Thursdays off.

"Looks like fun — is there room for one more?"

I recognized the voice instantly, and as I turned, I felt like an armadillo on the interstate. It was bad enough that she had come here, but what made it worse was that Grant was anal about putting us in boy-girl order for the back scratch, and I happened to be scratching Roxanne. In the *Handbook of Boy-friends and Girlfriends*, this particular scenario was probably on the page labeled "Crash and Burn." The only saving grace was that I was still wearing Paula's cap. Call me sentimental, but I always put it on first thing in the morning and didn't take it off until I went to bed.

Until that point, we were all making idle conversation about the little captions of information that Grant gave us on everything from the history of the known universe to what interplanetary toilets looked like. But the second Paula made her appearance, conversation stopped dead. What eyes didn't turn to her purposely turned away, and a pall fell over the room like a dense layer of fog. It was like in one of those bad westerns when the villain bursts in through the swinging doors of the saloon.

I got up and approached her, feeling about as uncomfortable and awkward as a being could get, human or otherwise.

"Hey," I said, "you're . . . here."

Grant, on the other hand, was lizard-smooth. "Miss Quinn!" he said, acting pleased to see her. "Come sit down — I'm sure Jason would love to scratch your back."

In a usual crowd, that would have dragged forth at least a half dozen snickers, but this was not your usual crowd. Everyone just silently waited to see what happened next. There was no welcome mat at this party.

"That's okay — we'll go outside," I told Grant. Then I took her hand and led her out.

Once we were outside, and out of view of the scratching mob, I tried to make small talk, but Paula wasn't buying.

"So you never come to Old Town, huh?"

"I didn't before," I answered honestly. "But I guess it kind of grows on you."

"Yeah, like athlete's foot."

"So how did you know I was here?" I asked.

"I didn't. I was coming to get that picture that looks like Billy, and then I heard voices," she said with a smirk. "Somehow I knew it wasn't ghosts."

My shoulders started itching something crazy, and I thought to ask Paula to scratch them for me, but somehow I didn't think it was appropriate at the time.

The door creaked open behind me, and Grant stepped out.

"So you're the scoutmaster?" Paula said, turning to him.

"Scoutmaster and den mother all rolled into one," he responded.

"We're all just a bunch of happy campers," I said with a forced smile.

"If you're scouts," asked Paula, "where are the uniforms?"

"It's a camp run by our church," Grant said calmly. "Jason was probably too embarrassed to tell you that he came."

"My parents made me," I offered.

"Were you here twenty years ago, Mr. Grant?" asked Paula. I began to get the test sweats, which usually only accompanied midterms and finals.

"Here in Old Town?" Grant asked. "Sure, I lived right up the street."

"Good, because I have a few questions I'd like to ask you."

I leaned over and whispered in Paula's ear, "C'mon, Paula, don't embarrass him."

But Grant, who overheard me, said, "No, I'd be happy to answer your questions. I'm kind of an expert on Old Town."

"Okay . . . ," said Paula. I could see her heading straight for the jugular — it was a trait I was fond of, but damn it, why did she have to express it now? "Who owned that house over there?" she asked, pointing to the peeling green house we had explored a few weeks ago, in another lifetime.

"The Chambers lived there," he told her, point blank. "Years ago, of course. As I recall, Billy had a brother who died before he was born."

"Flu?" asked Paula.

"No, car accident," answered Grant. "His folks say that Billy is the spitting image of him."

"Too bad," I shoved in, with a stupid, nervous chuckle.

"Okay . . . ," said Paula, letting loose her second offensive, "what about the message on the pantry door?"

Grant had obviously never seen it.

"It says GOD HELP US," I prompted. "It's carved into the wood."

"Hmm, that's certainly odd," he said. "Well, Mr. Chambers was known to drink too much around the time their first son died — maybe that has something to do with it. Or else it might have been the infestation. People went a little bit nuts over that."

"Infestation?" I said — now I was becoming interested in Grant's little fiction.

"Spiders," said Grant. "Brown recluse spiders. Thousands of them. They were everywhere. Their bite could swell you up like a balloon — they're more poisonous than black widows, you know."

Paula squirmed just a bit.

"Exterminators came and dusted the place with so much pesticide," said Grant, "that the ground became toxic. It took years until the rains washed it out."

I watched Paula. What had begun as distrust and doubt was inching toward belief and acceptance. "And that was the epidemic?"

"If you could call it that."

"People died?"

"Not many," said Grant. "The elderly mostly. Some from the spider bites, and others may have gotten too much pesticide — although it was never proven. In any case, the pesticide company paid a whole lot of money to keep us quiet about what happened."

"You got paid, too?" asked Paula.

Grant smiled. "Bought a brand-new house and a satellite dish," he said.

I laughed at that. Paula had no idea why I would find that funny, and she looked at me like I was from Mars. Close, but no cigar.

"You know," she said to Grant, "that really stinks, taking money like that."

Grant looked a bit embarrassed about it. "Well, I guess even in a town like this, money talks. It's not something we're proud of. People don't like to talk about it."

"So I've noticed." Paula eyed him a moment more, and I could see the exact instant when she decided he was telling the truth. I was impressed that Grant could do such a thing, yet furious at him for duping Paula so completely. I couldn't stand to see her fooled, and I hated the fact that I couldn't contradict the story.

Paula folded her arms and tried one last attempt. "How about the BB glove?" she asked.

Grant blinked uncomprehendingly. "Sorry," he said. "I have no idea what you're talking about."

"Can I take some time to walk her back?" I asked, changing the subject real fast.

He gripped me firmly on my itching shoulder, in that warm way he had, and said, "As long as you're back in time for dinner."

"Dinner?" said Paula incredulously. "He gives you dinner?"

I shrugged. "It's kind of a three-meal plan."

We walked back, taking the road that led to the washed-out bridge.

Paula laughed out loud. "Pesticides!" she said. "Spiders and pesticides! What a way to screw up a small town." She turned to me. "He's telling the truth, isn't he?"

I couldn't look at her. "Don't ask me," I said.

Soon the dead trees around us gave way to huge oaks outside the irradiated perimeter. "So this is what your doing all summer?"

"It's not so bad," I told her. "It keeps me out of trouble."

"Looks like it keeps you in shape, too," she said, poking my pectorals, which felt tight, and a bit sore. I assumed it was from all the exercise Grant had us do. I was kind of pleased that Paula noticed.

"Yeah," I said. "Maybe next year I'll go out for baseball again."

She smiled at that.

We reached the broken bridge, then climbed down the slope to the dry creek bed and up the other side. "Do you think you could skip out on Camp Grant every once in a while?" she asked. "Because my parents want to have you over for dinner. They want to see with their own eyes what a menace to society you really are."

"Oh, boy," I said. "Maybe I should go out and get an earring just for the occasion."

She laughed. Then I got a bit serious.

"Maybe," I said, "you could really shock them, and tell them that . . . I wasn't actually human."

She laughed even louder. "Oh, they'll love that. Dating outside of my species!"

We grinned dumbly at each other for a few seconds, I kissed her, and then she turned to go. She never knew how close I came to telling her the truth.

When I got back to the diner, the scratching session was over and Grant was out back, tending to the generator. I thought I was lucky that I didn't have to face him right away. I was wrong. As I entered, that pall fell again, as if everyone had been talking about me while I was gone. Not even Wesley would look me in the face.

Billy Chambers was the first to say something.

"Lucky for you," he said, "Grant knows how to unscrew a situation." Clearly they had eavesdropped into everything that had gone on outside.

"She won't come by here again," I told him. "You don't have to worry."

Billy just shrugged as he sketched more of his graphite demons on a scrap of paper. "I didn't know you were still going out with her."

"Why, are you jealous?" I asked snidely. "You were the one who broke up with her, remember."

Then it started coming at me in stereo. Roxanne spoke up. "Y'know," she said, "I see them together all the time. I saw them at the movies just the other day."

Wesley leapt to my defense. "What's wrong with going to the movies? Everyone goes to the movies."

"It's okay," I told him. "I can take care of this myself."

I looked around the room. There was uncertainty on everyone's faces. They could tell a line was being drawn in the sand, and they didn't know which side to stand on.

"If you've got a problem with me going out with Paula," I told Billy and Roxanne, "then it's *your* problem, not mine."

Billy stood up. "It's everyone's problem," he announced. "If she figures things out, she could blab it to the whole town."

"She's smart, but she's not a mind reader. She won't figure it out." But even as I said it, I knew that this wasn't what they were really getting at — and I got mad, because I realized what was coming next.

"We're not supposed to be around them," growled Billy. "And we're definitely not supposed to be dating them."

I gritted my teeth and spat my words at him: "Paula is not a *them.*"

"Whatever," he said, glaring at me through his mottled gray eyes.

A sensible person would have backed off at that point, but I guess I wasn't the sensible type. I wanted to make him as angry as he had made me.

"You know, Billy," I said. "There's a picture that looks just like you hanging on a wall down the street."

Billy snapped his eyes up to me. "Yeah, so?"

"So I guess you were last in line when they were handing out faces, huh, Billy-boy?"

A bunch of the other kids laughed. Billy's under-average features got all sharp, and his lips stuck out in anger. "Are you calling me ugly, Miller?" he snarled.

I shrugged and grinned. "Face it, Billy, your parents didn't exactly pick you out a set of designer genes, now, did they?"

More snickers. Billy's pale, freckled face turned a deep crimson. "Well," he said, "at least I don't go dating something like Paula Quinn. But I guess you have a thing for inferiority."

I lost it. I knew I would. He could say what he liked about me, but saying things about Paula — that was walking into a minefield. I dove on Billy, swinging with no mercy, and he fought just as furiously. Around us the kids all stood up and spread back, forming that little arena that always surrounds a good fight.

I hurled him back against the wall, then threw a jab at his nose, but he ducked at the last second. My fist hit the wall . . .

. . . and went through it.

I pulled my hand out with a cloud of sawdust. It wasn't a plasterboard wall — it was wood. Seeing the hole in the wall sort of gave us both pause. My hand didn't hurt, although I knew that it should have.

"That'll be enough!" It was Grant. I turned to see him storming toward me across the floor.

Billy and I stared at each other with those don't-turn-your-back sort of eyes.

"That could have been your head," I told him.

The other kids looked at the hole and were impressed. I

really didn't want them to be impressed — my little antisocial fighting streak was more of an embarrassment to me than anything else.

Grant grabbed me solidly by the arm. "A word outside, Jason." He pulled me out to the front porch, while behind me, I heard Wesley say, "Y'know, Billy, you gotta admit he's right — you're kind of like the dog-faced boy of Billington."

"Aw, shut up."

Grant was stern with me, but he held his temper on a tight leash. More than I could say for myself. "As your father's son, I expect you to set an example," he said.

"And what's that supposed to mean?"

"It means that fighting with Billy Chambers is counterproductive."

"But he said —"

"What he said was probably right," concluded Grant.

I could feel my hands balling into fists at my side again. "Now *you're* gonna tell me I can't see Paula Quinn?"

Grant chose his words carefully. "It would be wise . . . ," he said, "if you just let it go. In case you haven't noticed, there are plenty of girls right here who like you."

This was news to me, although I had to admit I wasn't looking very hard. "Not interested," I told him, "and besides, there's nothing to worry about with Paula."

"No? She found out about the glove, didn't she?"

I looked down and kicked up some dust. "I showed it to her before I knew anything — and if *you* hadn't been so secretive about the whole thing, I might have kept it to myself."

"The kids here follow your lead, Jason," added Grant — which was also news to me. "What do you think is going to happen if you continue going out with her?"

"I think they'll realize that while we're waiting for this phantom invasion, we still have to live."

Grant took a deep breath — I could feel his temper tugging at that leash. "You're going to have to break away from her in a couple of weeks anyway," he said. "No matter what."

"Why?" I demanded, wondering what other news he was about to blindside us with.

He took a moment to think about his response and finally said, "You'll have to find that out for yourself." And so ended today's ration of information.

Grant might have been put in charge of us, but he didn't own me.

"No," I said, and repeated it, just in case there was a part of the word he didn't understand. "No, I won't stop seeing Paula." Then I turned my back on him and stormed off.

"Where are you going?" he yelled after me.

"Anywhere but here!" I shouted. "And if you have a problem with it, go tell my parents. Then maybe at least they'll visit."

10

Night of the Becoming

What happened next had to come eventually — we just pushed it a little, that's all. The fact was, that no matter how high Grant chose to build his dam, the things he was keeping from us had to burst through.

After my fight with Billy Chambers and then with Grant, I refused to sit alone to stew about it. So I invited Paula over for dinner. She arrived at dusk.

"I guess Grant wasn't cooking anything good tonight," she said as she stepped in.

I shrugged. "Nothing like a home-cooked meal."

She looked around at the house, which I had struggled hard to clean before her arrival. "Where are your parents?"

"Well, that's the thing," I told her. "It's kind of just you and me."

"But I thought you were inviting me over for dinner with them."

"Don't you think I can cook?"

She looked at me doubtfully and a bit apprehensively.

"What's the problem?" I said. "It's not like it's a 'romantic' dinner or anything — I just thought it would be nice, to, y'know . . . eat."

"Are your parents out of town?" she asked, always the investigator.

In town, but out to lunch was what I wanted to say. "They're just out," I said.

I pulled out a chair for her, figuring I might as well be a gentleman whether she liked it or not. Then I ran off into the kitchen to get the two plates I had already prepared.

There's only so much you can do with frozen dinners. True, I had scooped their steaming contents out of the little black trays and onto our good china, then sculpted it so that it presented well — but Salisbury steak is Salisbury steak.

"Home-cooked?" she questioned.

"Well, how about home-nuked?"

I watched as she moved her fork around in her potatoes. There was something so wonderful about having put that meal together and then just sitting there with her. It made all of my troubled thoughts just slink into the closet and stay there. I didn't have to think about it — I could pretend, just for a little while, that it didn't exist, and I knew it would be like that for as long as she stayed.

But before either of us raised a fork to our mouths, the phone rang. I let the machine get it, and it turned out to be Wesley. I leapt up from the table, knocking down my chair, and raced to the phone, terrified that he might blather something out loud that I'd never be able to explain to Paula.

"Yeah, yeah, I'm here," I said as I picked up the phone and shut down the machine.

"Jason," he said, "I think we're in trouble." Wesley didn't sound too good.

I glanced at Paula and smiled before I returned to the conversation. "What kind of trouble?" I asked.

"The worst" was his answer. "How do you feel?"

"The same as usual," I said.

"Me, too. My shoulders keep peeling like a sunburn, and my joints keep aching."

"Yeah, so?" I knew the symptoms of the new treatment as well as he did. If I could stand it, then so could he.

"But there's something else I didn't notice before. . . ." His voice was sounding real thick now, as if he were crying. "Jason, my hair is falling out."

"What? No! What?"

Paula looked up at me. I smiled at her again, then ducked into the kitchen.

"What are you talking about? Your hair looked fine today."

"Not the hair on my head, but the other places — my chest, under my arms. Even those little hairs on my knuckles."

"You gotta be kidding me!" I glanced out to Paula, who was listening to my side of the conversation, trying to fill in what Wesley might be saying. "I'm sorry, I can't talk now," I told him.

"Then don't talk; listen. Listen to everything I say, and don't shut me up until I'm done."

"Okay, then talk."

He cleared his throat. "I figured there had to be a reason why our parents were leaving us alone — and I kept thinking about it and thinking about it. That's when I noticed the thing about the hair. Then I get to thinking about this whole mission of theirs. If they have to take up where they left off twenty years ago, then it means it's like we were never born. I don't think we were ever *supposed* to be born."

I heard him breathe heavily on the other end a few times. I could feel his fear across the phone line. "Jason, I think they're killing us."

I let his words hit me — I let them bounce around, weighed them with both fear and logic, and compared them against my own observations. And I came to the conclusion that Wesley's little equation must have spat out the wrong answer.

"No, it can't be," I told him. "I mean, why would Grant be spending so much time and energy training us?"

"To keep us busy?" suggested Wesley. "To keep us out of the way?"

"No, Wes, that would be — it would be *counterproductive.* They wouldn't do that."

"Well, *we* think they might," Wesley said.

"We?"

"I talked to some of the others when we left Old Town today, and showed them my hair problem. They were all scared like me."

I paced back and forth, and dared to touch my own eyebrows. A few short hairs came off on my fingertips, and I tried to tell myself that it didn't mean anything. "But my father's in charge!" I whispered, trying to keep Paula from hearing. "If he's calling the shots, then nothing bad will happen to us."

"How much do you trust your father?" Wesley asked.

That was one answer I didn't even have to think about. No matter how many lies he had told me — no matter what he had done to hide the truth, in my whole life he had never done anything to hurt me.

"Something's missing," I told him. "You're jumping to conclusions. You'll start a panic!"

But it was too late to stop that. There was a knock on the door, and I told Wesley to hold on. It was Ford-called-Ferrari. He was a regular at my "slumber party." In fact, there were over a dozen regulars now, every night. I don't know why they all decided to come to my house, but each night, more and more kids just showed up with their sleeping bags and pillows — although they usually didn't start showing up until later.

"Jason, I'm really scared," he said as he barged his way in. "We gotta do something before it's too late!"

I shushed him, and when he turned to see Paula, he said, "Uh-oh."

Paula, who must have heard fragments of my talk with Wesley, had now heard this little dramatic excerpt as well.

"What's been going on around here?"

"Church stuff, okay?" I offered.

When Paula looked around, I could tell she noticed the sleeping bags that were shoved into various corners of the living room, not hidden as well as I thought. She turned to me and didn't even ask. She just waited for me to answer.

I opened my mouth, fishing for a truth I could get away with, but there was another knock on the door. It was little Amy. By the look on her face, I could tell she had been crying. As I looked out of the window, I saw a few more kids coming. Some on bikes, some just running, and all gripping their training gloves like security blankets.

I picked up the phone again. "Wesley, how many kids did you talk to?"

"Most of them," he answered. "All of them."

I brushed my fingers nervously through my hair, the way my father did. "Okay, okay, I want you to find everyone and get them to my house *now!*" Although it seemed that most of them were already on their way.

The screen door opened, and more kids came in. "Hi! You remember Paula," I said before they could open their mouths and say a word. They all just filed in silently when they saw her, trying lamely to hide their training gloves.

"Looks like the campers aren't as happy as you thought," she said.

I started to get mad, but I refused to take it out on her.

"I guess I really have to take care of this," I said apologetically.

"Why didn't you tell me there were more of those gloves around?" she said, her suspicion climbing.

I couldn't stand her looking at me like that, so I grabbed my own glove down from the shelf and held it out to her. "Here, you want one?" I said in my frustration. "Go ahead, take it."

But, of course, she didn't. We both knew it wasn't a glove she wanted.

"Paula," I said, "I promise, as soon as I know what this is all about, I will tell you *everything.*" I meant what I said, and I didn't care if the other kids heard.

She reluctantly accepted my promise. "I don't like this 'camp' of yours," she said, then shoved a whole Salisbury steak into her mouth and left, chewing.

Once she was gone, I sat everyone down and tried to calm their fears, but as more and more arrived, the gathering began to feel like a wake. The house was filled with an oppressive air of misery and terror.

By nine they had all arrived — even Billy and Roxanne were there, although they stayed in the back and said nothing to me.

As I stood before them, Grant's words suddenly came back to me: *The kids here follow your lead, Jason.* And I wondered if they knew that it was the blind leading the blind.

"Okay, first thing," I announced. "We . . . are . . . *not* . . . dying."

Most of them sighed an amazing breath of relief, as if my saying it made it true.

"Do you know that for a fact?" someone challenged.

"I know what I know," I told them. Which was nothing.

It was Ferrari who switched us onto the right track. He raised his hand timidly. "Jason," he said, "do I look different to you?"

"Huh?"

"You know, do I look different — do I look *funny?* Because I don't think I look like I'm supposed to. . . ."

To be honest, I had never looked close enough to notice. He looked kind of pale, but that was probably just from being scared. I scratched his shoulder gently. "You're okay, Ferrari — there's nothing to worry about."

"How about my eyes — how do they look?"

I peered at them and couldn't find anything wrong. "Blue," I said with a shrug. "They look blue."

"Yeah," said Ferrari, "but my eyes are brown."

The other kids began to lean around to get a good look at Ferrari's eyes.

"Maybe it's just the light," suggested Wesley.

But no amount of light could make brown eyes do that.

I stepped over to the mirror in the hallway and looked at my

100

own eyes. They were blue — but then they were always blue. They looked no different to me. It was my eyebrows that didn't quite seem right. They seemed . . . thinner. And as I brushed my finger across them again, a few more strands of eyebrow hair came loose.

On an impulse, I pulled off my shirt. My shoulders were peeling and raw, as were my back and my neck. I already knew about that. But then I took a long look at my chest. I didn't have many chest hairs to begin with, so it was hard to notice the difference, but I did notice something else. Those pecs that Paula had commented on earlier — they were bigger, but not just that. In some imperceptible way, they didn't look exactly . . . right. Something in their shape or their angle was off.

It was all enough for me to start drawing conclusions of my own, and I knew that this time the answer to the equation was right.

"Is that why we came here, to watch him admire himself?" said Billy, still pretty sore about that afternoon.

I wanted to fire something back at him but held down the urge. Instead, I quietly slipped my shirt back on, took a deep, deep breath, and approached the group. I stood before them, knowing what I had to say but not knowing how to say it.

"Those shots they're giving us," I began. "I don't think they're keeping us human." And from there, I let them start looking at their own bodies for the rest of the answer.

The simple truth was, we were slowly becoming ourselves.

If you've ever seen those movies where the marauding towns-folk head up the hill to Frankenstein's castle with pitchforks and torches, then you can imagine what it was like when two dozen kids marched with flashlights and iron gloves toward the only house in Billington with a satellite dish pointing north.

As we approached, I could see Grant's silhouette in the kitchen window. I would have loved to have seen his face the moment he caught sight of us, but all I could see were shadows. He disappeared from view, and a few moments later, the garage door began to crank itself open. Grant stood there in the empty garage. If our arrival unnerved him, he didn't show it — he kept in calm control.

What struck me first was the garage itself. Twenty years of living human, and yet the garage was bare. There was a rake, a spade, and that was about it — no boxes of things too special to ever throw out, no old furniture — as if nothing over the past two decades had been worth holding on to.

"To what do I owe this visit?" he asked.

I took a step forward from the crowd. "You know why we're here." I maintained the same calm control over my own voice. "Did you think we wouldn't figure out what was happening to us?"

He smiled. "I assumed you would," he said, "but I'm impressed that you realized it so soon!"

Seeing that smile just made me angry. I didn't know what to do, so I raised my glove and aimed it at him. In turn, he raised his own hand, clicked his remote, and the garage door cranked down behind us.

"If you're going to riddle me with ball bearings, by all means go ahead. But if you don't intend to shoot, I suggest you put your arm down."

No, I wasn't going to shoot him. I slowly lowered my arm.

"You still haven't grasped how fortunate you are," he told us.

"You keep saying that," I reminded, "but you haven't shown anything to prove it." I began to feel the control in my voice slipping toward rage. "Now it's time to put up or shut up."

I could hear the others rumble their approval behind me. I took another step forward — not quite in his face but close. "You're going to tell us everything," I demanded, "and you're going to tell us now."

"Or else?"

"Or else you lose," I told him. "You lose everything you've worked for. You lose our attention and our respect. You lose *us*." Then I pulled the glove off of my hand and cast it down at his feet.

Grant regarded us with the sternest face he could muster. He looked out over all the others. "Does he speak for all of you?"

Although I had my eyes fixed on Grant, I heard the response. First one at a time, and then a clattering rush of everyone's gloves hitting the concrete, like a sudden downpour of rain. When the silence returned, Grant looked to the back, to Billy Chambers.

"Billy," said Grant, "does Jason speak for you?"

Billy, who still had his glove, took a moment to consider it. He was looking at me, not Grant. There was a lot of anger toward me in those eyes. But I suppose some things are stronger than anger.

"Yes," said Billy, ripping his glove off of his hand and dropping it to the ground. "Yes, he does."

I turned to Grant again, thinking him beaten — or at least humbled — by our defiance.

But then he began to smile. Not coldly, not apologetically,

but broadly — and then he let loose a laugh that sounded inappropriately joyful. He slapped his hand down on my itching shoulder.

"Good!" he said. "Then you've proven yourselves."

"What? What are you talking about?" I demanded, but he didn't answer me. Still gripping my shoulder, he turned me to face the others and addressed them, not me.

"Jason Miller has united you all in a single purpose," he announced boldly. "He has brought you together with one mind, one goal. You will therefore answer to *him* now. I will still be responsible for your care and training, but in everything else, you will answer to Jason."

Everyone looked at one another, trying to fathom this new spin our confrontation had taken.

"And if we don't?" challenged Roxanne.

"There is no 'if,' " answered Grant. "You *will*."

The group began to murmur. Some of them sounded pleased, others uncertain, but there were no further challenges. My nomination had been approved.

The rage that had carried me into the garage had been doused so effectively, I could only stand there dumbfounded and limp-willed as I stared at Grant.

"But . . . but . . ."

"Congratulations, Jason," Grant said, beaming. "I knew it would be you."

"But . . . what about this afternoon? What about . . . me and Paula?"

Without taking his eyes off of me, he said, "Your decisions will be their decisions now. Your choices their choices. I will no longer question the decisions you make." And that's all he said about it. I realized that he had just officially handed me a huge scepter of power, and yet I suddenly felt more powerless than I'd ever felt before.

Grant turned again to the others. "From now on, there will be no secrets between us," he proclaimed. "What I know, I tell to Jason, and what he knows, he tells to you."

It was as if Grant had harpooned me, deflating my rage. In one smooth motion, he had permanently skewered me between himself and my friends. Grant looked at me as if I should be proud to now be the Conduit of All Information, as indispensable as him in the scheme of things. It made me think of my father and that night when he took me to the ship, pouring out his confession. I wished I could have talked to him now — because now I understood what it was like to be impaled upon your mission.

"I can tell you what you'll look like," Grant announced with a sparkle in his eye. The offer brought the group to silence. Suddenly you could hear the crickets.

I didn't know about everyone else, but my own curiosity had drowned in the flood of my new responsibility. "Maybe . . . maybe we're not ready," I whispered to him.

"You'll never be ready," he responded, "but I'll show you anyway. You alone, Jason — and then you can decide if the others should see."

I nodded my numb acceptance.

While the others milled around the garage anxiously waiting, Grant led me inside his house. I forced myself to follow even though I knew that my brain was kind of running on fumes. He led me through his spotless, spartan home and down the narrow stairs into the dimly lit bowels of his basement.

As bare as his home was, his basement was an unparalleled clutter. It was full of things he had obviously scavenged from the ship. I saw more training gloves, which he must have been saving for the younger kids when they came of age, but nothing else I saw made sense to me. The place was stacked with artifacts strangely shaped and unnaturally textured, and I began to wonder how I could ever learn to live in a culture whose simplest objects had me stymied.

The basement itself seemed larger than the house above, as if it stretched out beneath the yard. We came around another stack of exotic clutter, then finally reached a door, as ordinary looking as any. Grant grasped the knob, turned to me, and said, "In your life, you're going to have many moments of glory. But this moment will stand above all others."

And with that, he slowly pushed the door open.

Years ago, there was this blind kid in our neighborhood. He had been blind from birth, and managed to get around in the land of the seeing pretty well, even for a kid. Since he didn't mind talking about being blind, a bunch of us would sit around and explain to him what things looked like. I tried to explain to him the color blue — but the only words I could use spoke of texture, or smell, or sound, or taste.

How can you describe something that you couldn't imagine before you saw it? Something so wholly different that imagination itself hadn't evolved far enough to grasp it?

That's the way it was when Grant led me into that room, for it wasn't a picture he had brought me in to see. . . .

It was one of them.

My heart pounded out a long drumroll before I could will

myself to move closer to it. The creature was both beautiful and frightening, savage yet godlike, as it lay motionless — lifeless — on a stone slab. Grant was right. Nothing could have prepared us.

"Do you see," said Grant, "why I couldn't tell you?"

As I gazed upon it, I thought about how I might describe it to the others, and realized that it simply wasn't possible. Sure, I could talk about its humanoid shape — but its form was far more perfect than any human I'd ever seen. I could say how incredibly muscular it was, and yet, how could I explain how something so strong and dense could seem almost weightless? I could tell them that its skin looked like pure, pure peach marble, swirling with rivers of perfect color — but then they wouldn't understand its softness, and how you could almost feel that softness against your eyes as you gazed at it. And I could try to give the others an image of its dazzling thick mane of hair, which grew not only from its head but also from its shoulders, tapering down to the small of its back, but I'd have no words to use when I tried to describe its color. The closest I could come would be to say that its gossamer hair had no color of its own but seemed to drag the colors out of the air, looking golden blond one moment, then ice blue or flame red the next. It refracted the light with such breathtaking magnificence, you'd think it was spun from diamond thread.

I could feel my knees growing weak as I looked at it, my brain trying to come to terms with the creature stretched out before me.

That's when it opened its eyes.

I yelped and jumped back, but Grant was there to catch me. "It's all right," he said.

The creature sat up and looked at me. The features of its face were strong, yet angelic, from the smooth curves of its nose and chin to the clarity of its deep green eyes, unfettered by lashes or brows. Those eyes were hypnotic, but more than that, they were deep. Deep enough to fall into.

As it looked at me, the corners of its mouth turned up in a smile.

"Jason!" it said. "Oh, man, I thought I'd never see you again!"

I'm glad Grant was still holding me up, because my legs had forgotten how. I could only gape in astonishment as the realization spun through my brain and out of my mouth in the form of a single word. A name.

"Ethan?"

11

Man of the Hour

"I almost died," said Ethan. "It hurt more than anything you can imagine."

I couldn't look at him as he talked. I still couldn't reconcile his overpowering image coupled with a voice that sounded almost the same — only fuller and more resonant, as if his lungs were twice as big. He was shirtless but wore a pair of Levis, which I guess was perfectly natural but somehow seemed entirely absurd — like those frogs they shellac and dress up like golfers.

"I felt it at first in my gut," Ethan continued, "like I had eaten something really bad, but then it spread to my arms and legs. I felt like I was boiling on the inside. The pain got worse and worse, and then I just blacked out. My parents say that I was in a coma for two weeks and almost didn't make it. I was all swollen and bruised . . . but bit by bit the swelling started to go away. And when I woke up, I looked like this. My parents had a lot of explaining to do."

He took a long look at me. For the most part, I looked pretty much the same as I did before Ethan "died." "You're lucky it's happening to you slowly," he said, "under Doc Fuller's control."

Behind me, Grant reminded me that we had a garageful of anxious kids. "What do you want to do?" he asked me.

I forced myself to look at Ethan again. A shiver of awe slid down my spine. "You look pretty damn incredible. You know that, don't you?" I told him.

"What can I say?" said Ethan. "I'm a stud in any gene pool."

I laughed at that. Then I felt my shoulders itching again. When I reached inside my shirt to scratch, I could swear I felt the faintest hint of velvety peach fuzz there. It was weird and wonderful.

"We'll bring him to the others," I told Grant. "That is, if he wants to go."

The Ethan-thing looked down at his thin perfect fingers and wrung them nervously in his lap, then looked up to me with his riveting eyes. "Sure — got a giant cake I can pop out of?"

We came back through the house, and I opened the door that led to the garage. By the look on my face, they all must have realized that they were in for something major. I stepped in, Grant followed, and then a moment later Ethan apprehensively crossed the threshold.

There were gasps, and everyone backed away in a silence.

"Everybody," I said, "I'd like to re-introduce you to a friend."

Ethan looked around and fixed his eyes on his sister. Then he strode toward her with powerful yet light-footed steps.

When Amy realized that she was the target of his attention, she backed up against the wall and gripped onto Ferrari, who was standing next to her.

Ethan knelt down before her, looked into her eyes, and

110

smiled. That unearthly smile had so much power that it sliced right through Amy's fear, turning it to wonder. She slowly released her hand from the death grip she had on Ferrari, then reached out and dared to touch the face before her. When she stroked his cheek, she let out something that was a cross between a gasp and a laugh. "It's so beautiful," she said.

Ethan's smile widened, and he said gently, "So are you, Aimsie."

Amy withdrew her hand, and her expression changed into a bewildered shock. No one but Ethan called her Aimsie — and everyone knew that.

A whisper shot through the garage like wind through a wheat field: *"It's Ethan, it'sEthanit'sEthanit'sEthan. . . ."*

I could see in Amy's face and her body language that there was a battle going on inside of her. One part of her wanted to deny it and run away, screaming, while another part of her wanted to embrace her mystically transformed brother. It was that part that finally won the battle. She threw herself into Ethan's arms and hugged him tightly, clinging onto his soft, diamond-thread hair. She wept tears of confused emotion — and she wasn't the only one. I could hear sniffles around the room and see the quivering chins.

Roxanne came forward next — no runny mascara to intensify her tears.

She reached out and touched him. Then one by one, they all moved forward and touched his skin, his hair, and his face, until he began to laugh out loud from the feel of their caresses.

I arrived home with an entourage of kids who were in no state of mind to return alone to their homes. My parents were home when I got back that night, looking haggard and exhausted from their many weeks of tireless work. In fact, everyone's parents had gone home that night.

"Grant called," my dad explained, "and told us what was happening. I felt everyone ought to be with their kids tonight."

And so one by one parents arrived and took their kids home, to be a human family, if only for one last night.

When they were all gone, I went into my room. I had wanted to talk to my dad and tell him all the things burning through my head, but I couldn't bring myself to do it, so we barely said anything to each other.

As I sat at my desk, I found myself gazing at the crumbling picture of J.J. Pohl again. Then Mom stepped into the room.

"If you hate us for not telling you about Ethan, I wouldn't blame you," she said.

I shrugged. "How could you tell me? If I were you, I wouldn't tell me, either." I tried to hide the photo from her, but she saw it anyway.

"Are you going to keep it?" she asked.

"Nah," I said. After all, it was just a pointless glimpse of a lost future. I reached my hand out over the wastebasket, but try as I might, I couldn't make my fingers release the picture into the trash. So instead I shoved it into my desk drawer.

As I lay on my bed that night, Mom sponged down my itching back, the way she'd done all those years ago when I'd had the chicken pox. Dad peered in every once in a while but kept his distance from me. I felt closer to him than ever before, finally understanding what he must have been going through, and yet in spite of that closeness, a wall had come down between us.

Just before I nodded off to sleep, I asked Mom what it was that kept them busy sixteen hours a day, seven days a week. This time she didn't just give me a quick, pat answer.

"We have to pick strategically sound landing spots," she said. "We have to infiltrate major databases and computer networks without being noticed. We have to study different cultures and figure out how to use their weaknesses to our advantage. . . ."

There was more, but I made myself stop listening. I knew it was her voice, I knew they were her words, but hearing them spill from her mouth was just too disturbing. When did *What would you like for dinner?* and *How was your day at school?* turn into *How do we conquer the world?* To be honest, I wish she would have just said, "You don't want to know."

When she was done, she paused for a moment, considering her words, then added, "But that's not the only reason we've been gone, Jason." She put the sponge in the basin. "Where we come from, children don't really know their parents," she said. "They're raised by people like Grant. By staying away, we're trying to get back to the normal ways." She wrung out the sponge and continued to gently pat my back. "But maybe I can still be your mom for a while."

I closed my eyes. "I won't tell if you won't."

12

Bald-Faced Lies in the Circus of the Stars

"We all know what we have to do, and knowing puts us halfway there."

I told Paula that the reason everyone had been upset was that we'd thought one of the kids had fallen down an abandoned well — but we were mistaken. I wore dark glasses to cover my eyebrows, and I told her that my skin was looking different because I'd been getting too much sun. Then when she stopped by my house a few days later and saw me packing, I told her we were visiting a sick aunt out of state.

Lying to Paula, I discovered, was like learning to ride a bike. At first you're terrified, but the more you go along, the easier it gets. Although I think she suspected that I wasn't giving her everything, I don't think she knew how bald-faced the lies were. And so it was a long time until she had any idea that we had all picked up and moved into Old Town.

"We're strong and growing stronger. Each day we're getting better."

Most of our parents had inherited jobs that involved working with their hands, so they were pretty well equipped for a closed society. We had masons and carpenters, a plumber, a glazier, and even a mechanic, who brought a generator large enough to power the part of Old Town we planned to use.

We worked our way out from the diner, cleaning and repairing all the adjacent homes, until there were separate living quarters for the adults and the kids. I called them barracks, but Grant preferred to call them dormitories.

A perimeter fence came next, then windowless wooden corridors that connected each building — so that when our change was complete, we didn't have to risk being out in the open to get from place to place. Then only our parents, who would stay human until the ships arrived, would be seen by the outside world.

Building was easy, and as we were growing physically stronger than our parents, we became the backbone of the construction effort. We were all so full of ourselves and what we were doing that it began to feel like one big party — like an old-fashioned Amish barn raising.

"Isn't it great," Wesley said to me as we happily hammered side by side, "that we don't have to worry about things being boring anymore?"

"Things were boring?" I asked. To be honest, I couldn't remember.

"Look what we can do — it should have taken us a month to do this work, but we did it in a week!"

115

An article ran in the *Billington Bugle* saying that we were building a retreat open to any affiliated church in the state. We didn't mention that there *were* no affiliated churches. We openly invited the rest of the town to come help, but, like most towns, Billington had an age-old rivalry between local lodges and congregations. When it came to building big group projects, you didn't help the competition. And so our invitation guaranteed us being left alone.

When we returned to our old homes, we only went there to salvage. We took mattresses, chairs — only things that were useful — across a slipshod bridge we had built over the creek. The bridge would stand just long enough to get what we needed across, before we tore it down and isolated ourselves from the outside world. Isolation, it turns out, is not as difficult as you might think. Hidden in the oak grove, with the nearest homes almost a mile away, Old Town was out of sight and out of mind to the rest of Billington, as it had always been.

It was there, while we labored to build our compound, that we really began to change. I'm not talking about on the outside — I mean on the inside. The way we thought, the way we felt, and the way we looked at the world outside, as if we were watching from a telescope a million miles away. The thing about living in a private little world, is that you've got nothing to feed on but the same thoughts and ideas bouncing back at you from your friends. You sort of get locked in a feedback loop, and the things that start to sound normal and reasonable have no bearing on what's true. There's no ruler to measure truth, no scale to weigh right and wrong. All you have are the excited faces around you, waiting for judgment day.

"We've got a wild future ahead of us — can't you feel it?"

This time it was *me* who kept dishing out little captions of enthusiasm to keep us all focused and on task — and the more they listened, the more I believed what I said. Grant was terribly proud of me.

"It's our world now — perfect like us."

You could get drunk talking like that all the time.

By my own decree as Junior Fearless Leader, the "Transitionals," as Grant had started calling us, were all free to come and go from the compound as we pleased — that is, until we got too far along in our transition. I wanted them to know that they weren't prisoners. But none of them chose to go — not even me. Even though I wanted to see Paula, I pushed her to the very edge of my thoughts, convinced that it was the right and responsible thing to do.

Perhaps it was because Grant had a way of making us all believe that we were important in the grand scheme of things. As Grant's official Information Conduit, I felt especially important, because I got to sit in on some of the meetings. My parents were always there, and although they had spoken nothing but English to me all my life, in meetings they spoke the strange language of home, and Grant had to translate. There were so many layers of distance between me and my parents now, watching them was like watching strangers. But at least they still looked the same. The adults, who didn't have to worry about bursting out of their genes the way Ethan had, could maintain their human appearance as long as they had to.

Although I sat in on the meetings and kept up with all that was going on, I have to admit I didn't really enjoy them. I preferred my parents dull rather than devious.

As for the rest of our Loyal Order of Space Cadets, we started assigning them jobs that seemed steeped in significance. I say *we*, but it was Grant who assigned. He let me sit in and offer my opinions, but I don't think I affected any of his decisions. Ethan had already begun his studies in topics like relativistic quantum transduction and other stuff that his newly superiorized brain could handle better than we dim-witted Transitionals.

Wesley was being primed in navigation, which I guess was a good thing. I'd always thought that Wesley would have trouble navigating himself out of a shoe box filled with road maps, but in a few days, he was calculating complex coordinates in three dimensions, and maybe a few more I didn't know about.

Ferrari, Amy, and a few others got advanced training in a weird form of martial arts that involved parts of the body you never suspected could inflict damage, and Roxanne was taking an Alien-as-a-Second-Language course.

Everyone took pride in their tasks, and the pride soon grew so dense, it would take a machete to hack through it.

Billy Chambers's assignment was a fairly obvious one, being that he was the first one to graduate from his training glove to the real thing. Grant presented it to him even before our first week in Old Town was out. It was a fine metal mesh as sheer as a nylon stocking, and when he slipped it on, his entire arm glowed like a hot coal. The kids all oohed and aahed — it was another spectacle in our little circus. I don't know what fired out of its fingertips — the ammunition was invisible — but when Billy aimed his index finger at a tree, it melted a hole in the trunk the size of a baseball. *Melted*, not burned, as if the tree were made of plastic.

"Cool!" Billy had said. Then he had turned to me, smiling. "I'll bet you wish *you* were the first."

We gave Billy the job of enforcing rules for the Transitionals, and so he started to call himself Chief of Security. We also put him in charge of working with kids as they progressed from their training gloves to their real ones. For Billy, it was as good as making him the head of the National Rifle Association. He rose to the occasion, and before long we began to find holes melted in the strangest of places.

"Our old lives can't matter to us anymore. We have to see ourselves as we will be, not the way we used to be."

I dared to borrow Billy's glove one night while most everyone was asleep. It felt cold as I slipped my fingers into its soft, fine mesh, but it warmed up to my body temperature almost instantly. So fine was its lattice of filaments that it almost vanished when I had it on my hand. A flick of my pinky turned it on, and my hand glowed bright enough to light up the entire room. It felt strange — because it felt like I was wearing no glove at all. It would be easy to forget you were wearing it and to think all of that destructive power came from your fingertips and not from the capillaries of the otherworldly device. I turned it off and put it back on Billy's shelf. I had enough power for my tastes already. I could do without the Five Fingers of Death.

"Remember, we'll be the leaders when the others finally arrive, because they don't know this world the way we do."

On a clear night, Grant brought out a telescope, and he trained it on a dim star to the north. Astronomers hadn't even given the star a name, just a number. Grant told us *our* name for it, but it was this long thing with lots of consonants and no vowels, which I couldn't remember if you paid me.

With or without the telescope, the star was nothing more than a pinprick of light. It was hard to believe that something that appeared so small could have so great an impact on us.

"If you ever have any doubts, take a good look at Ethan. Would we have been created so beautiful if we weren't meant to have the world?"

When we went to bed after stargazing, Wesley said something that I couldn't get out of my head.

"You know," he whispered as the other kids were falling asleep, "if I had called everyone over to *my* house that night, instead of yours, it could have been me leading us over to Grant's. I could be the one in charge now — isn't that funny?"

"Why didn't you?" I asked.

He thought about it and shrugged. "I don't know. I should have been more like you that night."

He rolled over, and I could hear him snoring a few minutes later, but his thought kept me awake for a long time. What did it mean to "be like me"? *I* wasn't even like me anymore.

13

Sayonara, Señorita

If it weren't for Paula's cap, things might have gone a little bit differently — but the fact was, I still had it, and it was still on my mind way too often. I didn't dare wear it anymore — if I did, Billy Chambers, our local Security God, would have made my life unlivable. Can I help it if she hadn't given it to him? No, I wouldn't wear it, but I kept it under my pillow, and seeing it every night just before I went to bed turned it into a powerful ingredient in my nightmares.

My back had stopped itching by now, and the peach fuzz was becoming a velvet sheen. I was bursting out of my shirt with muscles, and while it all should have been a reason for rejoicing, I didn't feel too festive about it.

I was up late one night, comforting one of the little kids. There were only a half dozen of them, none younger than six, so it was finally decreed that they be spilled into our ranks as well. Of course they were duly terrified of Grant, and of Ethan, and of the fact that their little baby-toothed world had, in a way, taken on fangs. Everything seemed threatening to them, from the growth of the compound to their changing bodies — for they, too, were put into transition like the rest of us. And with our parents all forcing the distance between us, the littler kids cried themselves to sleep at night.

It became part of my job to comfort them. I would tell them a revamped version of the Warrior-Fools, but called them Warrior-Kings instead, and rather than becoming like the fragile people, *my* Warrior-Kings settled in to rule them. On this particular night, I was able to help the little girl to sleep, but my story didn't work for me, so I grabbed Paula's cap for comfort and ventured into the kitchen of our remodeled little house. Ethan, who only seemed to need several micro-seconds of sleep each night, was in his usual position at the table, studying. Tonight he pored over a history book in an incomprehensible language. He was like an older brother who had gone off to college and suddenly had nothing in common with me.

"It says here that we've been tooling around out there since Earth was in its Dark Ages," he told me. "You wouldn't believe some of the real estate we control."

I heard him but found myself not listening.

"You should read this stuff," he suggested.

I shrugged. "Sorry, I took Spanish."

He returned to his book, reading faster than I could turn pages.

"Ethan, when you first saw yourself," I asked, "how did you feel about it?"

Ethan dropped his brain out of light speed and looked at me. "I thought I was dead," he told me. "I thought I was an angel. Pretty stupid, huh?"

I looked at him closely. He was still spectacular to behold, but the image didn't fill me with awe the way it had when I first saw him. After a while, having him around just became . . . normal. It's kind of amazing the things we let become commonplace.

"Were you scared?" I asked.

"Are you kidding? I was terrified! If I hadn't thought I was already dead, I would have died of a coronary. But my parents were there to clue me in, so after a while I was okay."

"Do you . . . miss it?" I asked. "Do you miss the way you were?"

"I don't think about it," he answered. "We can do that, you know. Make ourselves not think about things, or feel things that are . . . well . . ."

"Counterproductive?" I suggested.

"Yeah."

He looked down at the pages before him, figuring I was probably done, but I knew I still hadn't found what I really wanted to ask. I wasn't exactly the Great Communicator — in fact, when it came to putting thoughts and feelings into words, I was on par with Wesley. Still, I knew that if I beat around the bush long enough, I'd scare up the way to say it. It only took a minute or two until it finally came to me.

"But — you're still *you!*" I said. "You look different, but it's still you!"

He stared at me with his piercing eyes, as if I had no clue. "Yeah, so? Why shouldn't I be me?"

"Because it's *human.*"

He glared at me, taking it as an insult. "Not even close," he said.

I could have pushed it, but I realized he'd already shut the thought out and bolted his mind behind it.

I looked down at Paula's cap, which I was fiddling with like rosary beads. Ethan noticed.

"I know what you're problem is," he said. "You've still got curveballs on the brain."

"Did your superior mind figure that one out?"

Ethan, I suppose, was the right person to be talking to when it came to girls. He'd been dating since the rest of us just whispered about girls behind their backs. Of course, Ethan was more known for his spectacular breakups than for actually going out with girls. Even here in the compound, he was up to his old tricks. Now that he was alive again, Roxanne had tried to pick up their relationship where they had left off, but Ethan snipped *that* fuse real quick. It hit her particularly hard, since it was probably the first time she had ever tried to date a nonhuman. She cried all the way back to the barracks and then went out to melt holes in things. Billy Chambers, of course, swooped in like a vulture, and the rest was history.

Ethan regarded me for a few moments, then smiled slyly. A sly smile on that strange face seemed doubly diabolical.

"You know, we could probably make Paula look like *us*," he said.

It caught me off guard. "Huh?"

"Sure we can — if they made us look human, I'll bet it works both ways. Get Doc Fuller to whip up a serum that wraps our DNA around hers, and *voilà* — problem solved."

Problem solved? What Ethan was suggesting was probably possible, and yet I knew it was wrong. Even if, by some stroke of amazing luck, Paula consented to it, it would still be wrong. No, it wasn't the solution — it was just a clever way of hiding the problem.

"Whadaya say?" asked Ethan. "I could talk to Grant about it — he's got a soft spot for me. He says I remind him of his brother."

"Thanks, but no thanks," I told Ethan. If anything, hearing him suggest it made my decision easier to make.

"Then you've gotta dump her," said Ethan, which was easy for him to say — he'd dumped Roxanne like she was a piece of junk mail on his doorstep, and it didn't disturb his microseconds of sleep in the least.

But Paula wasn't Roxanne. Roxanne had been fake even before she found out she really *was* fake. Paula, however, was brutally, painfully real. Saying good-bye to her, and all that went with her, was too difficult to imagine.

"Could you teach me how?" I asked Ethan.

He shrugged his powerful shoulders. "What's to teach? You look into her eyes, tell her you like her as a friend, and it's *Sayonara, señorita.*"

I heaved a heavy sigh. This was perhaps the easiest of all the things that lay ahead of me. If I couldn't handle this, how could I handle anything? How could I lead Grant's brigade? Did they know what a sniveling weakling I was?

"Don't worry about it," offered Ethan. "In two more months, you're going to look at her and find her totally repulsive. Believe me, I know."

I left to do the deed the next day.

It was late afternoon when I approached the compound

gate. The gate was never locked, but there was always some-one on guard to keep track of all comings and goings. It was a job assigned to an adult, just in case some quick talking and diplomacy was needed to turn away an unwanted visitor.

Today's guard was Pastor Bob, who used to preach long-winded sermons on love, peace, and everlasting flames. I wondered what he did these days.

The week before, as we'd been setting fence posts in con-crete together, I had asked him, "Do they have preachers where we come from?"

He had frowned in thought and answered, "Of a sort."

Then I had asked him if he still believed the things he'd spent the last twenty years preaching. I don't think he liked the question.

"We make adjustments," he had said, which would have been fine if he were a tailor, hemming my pants. I wondered how much of those beliefs had to be adjusted to make room for our new world order. I wondered if mine ever could — be-cause in spite of my years dozing through sermons and Sun-day school, I had developed some rudimentary moral compass, demagnetized though it might have been.

Now, as I approached Pastor Bob at the gate, he looked wor-ried, as though I might once again step on his spiritual hemline. When I showed him my training glove and told him that I was just going out for some target practice, his shoulders dropped in relief, and he was more than happy to pass me through.

As soon as the compound was out of view, I hid my glove be-neath some bushes, slipped on Paula's cap, and headed toward her house to fulfill my mission of pain.

* * *

"You're back!" said Paula, greeting me at the door. I could tell how glad she was to see me, but there was a touch of discomfort in her voice. A hurt that she was trying to hide. "How's your aunt?" she asked.

"Oh, better," I said, almost forgetting the lie I had told her. "I'm sorry I didn't call more. My dad got on my case about long-distance phone calls, you know?"

"It's okay," she said, though it really wasn't. "We said we wouldn't cling, right? You don't have to call me every five minutes."

Her dog, Mookie, was growling and snarling like a hell-hound as I stepped into the house.

Mr. and Mrs. Quinn peered out of the living room. "Hello, Jason," said Mrs. Quinn over the snarls. "You should have called — we would have had you over for dinner."

"Next time," I said, knowing full well there would be no next time.

The dog began to howl between snarls, and it finally oc-curred to me that it no longer understood my scent.

"Stop that, Mookie!" said Mrs. Quinn.

Mr. Quinn came over and shook my hand in that father-of-the-girlfriend sort of way. "Jason, I've been meaning to ask you — is your family involved with that retreat they're building in the woods?"

I should have been ready for the question, because Paula had warned me about her father. He was an optometrist who dreamed of being a private eye. I realized I was about to be scru-tinized beneath one of his finely ground lenses. "We've been away," I said, dodging the question.

"Dad, I told you, it's just a summer camp, okay? I saw it myself." Paula grabbed her backpack and tried to shepherd me out of the door.

"I'm just curious," said Mr. Quinn. He might have pushed harder, but Mookie let loose a barking conniption that distracted him long enough for Paula to drag me out.

"Wait a minute — where are we going?"

"It's bingo night," she informed me as we headed toward the street.

"You play bingo?"

"No, but I babysit for people who do. I figured you'd rather walk with me than be interrogated by my dad." And then she grinned. "Although the thought of leaving you there had crossed my mind."

I grinned as well, but the smile fell away as I remembered what I had come here to do. As we walked in the deepening twilight, I kept playing over and over in my head what I was going to say, how I was going to say it, and how I could keep from hating myself. All the while, she kept stealing glances at me, considering my face.

"What is it?" I asked, as if I didn't know.

"I don't know. Maybe I'm crazy, but you look . . . different, somehow."

It was now or never. I took her cap off my head, clutched it in my hands, and prepared to hand it back to her, with my sincerest apologies for being an asshole.

"It's your hair," she said. "That's what's different. It looks sort of brighter . . . thicker. What did you do to it?"

"Not much . . . ," I said.

She reached out and touched it. "It feels so soft. New shampoo?"

"Uh . . . special treatment."

"I like it."

This was unbearable. Without another thought, I launched into my planned speech. "Paula . . . y'see . . . while I was gone, I —"

"While you were gone, something really weird happened," she announced. "I've been dying to tell you about it."

I stuttered for a moment in the wake of my false start. "Wh-what happened?" I asked.

"I was in the mall," she began, "looking for clothes, when who do I see across the aisle but Ethan's parents. Turns out they're buying clothes, too."

"Yeah, so?"

"They're buying them in the Young Men's department."

I swallowed hard and played dumb. "Yeah, so?"

"So," said Paula, "I hear them talking. He wants to buy one pair of jeans, but she shakes her head and says, 'They're too tight for Ethan.' " Paula looked at me with raised eyebrows. "So what do you think of that?"

I slipped my hands into my pockets and picked up the pace. I felt myself beginning to drop into a deep, dark pit. "I think they must have gone nuts," I told her. "I mean, if your kid died like that, wouldn't you?"

"Yeah, but I wouldn't go shopping for summer fashions." She stopped and grabbed me by the arm. "Brace yourself, Jason — *I think Ethan might be alive!*"

"Don't be dumb," I said. "I was at the funeral."

"Did you check in the coffin?"

"Don't be sick!"

"All I'm saying is that if you didn't see him, then you can't be sure."

She stopped at a picket fence and opened the gate. "I'm gonna find out what's going on if it takes all summer."

I followed her to the front door. "Maybe you don't want to."

She looked at me and shook her head. "What are you afraid of?"

We stepped into a house that smelled of potpourri and Lemon Pledge. The living room was filled with antique furniture, and knickknacks arranged so perfectly they could have been glued in place. There was a foldout fence that blocked off the immaculate living room from the lethal hands of the toddler who had full run of the rest of the house.

"It's so nice of you to watch him for me, Priscilla," said the old woman who answered the door. "He's with me for a week, don'cha know. Still, I need my bingo to keep me sane." When she saw me come in behind Paula, she squinted at me dubiously and said, "Is this your brother?"

"A friend," she responded, "and it's Paula."

The woman nodded me a quick and scattered hello, then hurried off, muttering about her misplaced glasses.

The toddler looked up at me, said, "Ga-ga," then threw a truck at my feet.

"You don't have to stay," Paula said.

Still holding her cap in my hands, I said, "I won't stay for long, but there's something we need to talk about — I mean *really* need to talk about."

I guess my tone of voice finally got through to her. She shooed away the toddler, who continued to drop toys on me. "Something serious?"

I shrugged sadly. "Kind of."

From the next room came the sound of a drawer slamming. "Priscilla, dear, could you help me find my glasses?"

Paula turned and shouted, "Just a minute, Mrs. Pohl."

My brain did a violent and unexpected double take.

"Did you say . . . *Mrs. Pohl?*"

Paula steeled herself for whatever blow I was about to deliver. "So what do you have to tell me?"

But breaking up with Paula had suddenly slipped far from my mind as I realized who this old woman must be.

There are some moments in your life when all the forces that shape and define your being come into perfect focus and suddenly everything about your life just falls into place.

This was not one of those moments.

"Excuse me," I said, and made a beeline for the kitchen.

14

Remembering Me

In the brightly lit kitchen, the elderly woman rummaged through cabinets and drawers, searching for glasses that she probably needed glasses to find. I had to ask her the question. Even though I knew it was like poking myself in the eye, just to see if it would hurt, I had to ask.

"Are you related to J.J. Pohl?"

She stopped in mid-rummage and turned her farsighted eyes to me. "J.J. was my son," she said. "How do you know of him?"

The toddler wandered into the room, and I glanced over to see Paula entering behind him. She seemed more vulnerable and more uncertain than I had ever seen her. By now she must have known that I meant to break up with her. I turned back to the old woman.

"I — uh — heard he was a town hero."

"Oh, yes, J.J. sure is something — everybody loves J.J." said Mrs. Pohl, beaming at the thought of him. "He's in Vietnam, don'cha know, fighting the war."

There was a moment of uncomfortable silence.

"Mrs. Pohl," Paula said gently, "the war's been over for a long, long time."

Mrs. Pohl took in the information, reprocessed it, and corrected herself: "Yes . . . yes it has. And they gave J.J. a Medal of Honor when it was over, for what he did!"

"What did he do?" I asked.

"Well," she began, "a helicopter went down in the jungle. All that fire, and napalm everywhere. He went in, pulled a man out before it blew up, and carried him miles to safety." Then her face sobered a bit. "Terrible thing to go through all that, just to get sick and die at home a few years later."

She reached over and tickled the toddler under the chin. "This is my great-grandson — J.J.'s grandson. He's named after him — aren't you, Jason?" The toddler cooed, and I shifted uncomfortably.

"He's a Jason, too," Paula had to point out.

"Yeah, me and half the county," I grumbled.

She scowled at me, clueless as to why I had brushed that off.

The old woman smiled. "Would you like to see his medal?"

"Yeah," I said. "Yeah, I would."

"What about bingo?" Paula asked Mrs. Pohl.

"Oh, it'll still be there."

As she led us into the spotless living room, Paula turned to me and whispered, "What is it with you?"

Then, the second Paula turned her back, I reached over and grabbed the old woman's glasses, which were sitting on top of the microwave, and hid them deep in my pocket.

They say that when you die, your life flashes before your eyes. And now, as I felt the human part of me dying, it was J.J.'s life that was flashing before me.

Above the mantel was a wide wall covered with framed photos of him. J.J. and his family, J.J. with his bride, J.J. with his daughter, who must have been little Jason's mother. I had thought I would just see a medal — I hadn't expected to see a shrine.

"He kind of looks like you," Paula said to me — and then her face paled. There was a picture of J.J., black and white — must have been early sixties. He had a flattop butch and a broad smile. He must have been around fourteen, and there was no denying that it was me, right down to his smiling teeth. It ripped the wind right out of me — and must have hit Paula even harder. She just stared at the picture. Then she reached over and pushed my hair back off my forehead, to see how I might look with hair that short. She studied my face, then drew her hand back, unable to say a thing. I had always assumed that Paula had backup speech centers in her brain that kicked out clever lines in the thickest of situations. I never thought I'd see her speechless.

There was a lump in my throat as I took in the images before me. It was both horrible and wonderful. There were older pictures of his daughter on the wall, too. Even she looked like me.

Still, Mrs. Pohl had no idea. She reached up and pulled down a small wooden box from the mantel. Inside, on a velvet background, the Medal of Honor was pinned, still shining like new.

"President Nixon himself gave this to J.J.," she said, then pointed to a picture of Nixon shaking my hand. Paula was still looking back and forth at me and at the pictures, but her investigative instinct finally wrestled back her bewilderment.

"Exactly when did your son die?"

"Over twenty years ago." She shook her head sadly. "It was that awful, awful flu. It took some good people, it did. I can only thank the Almighty that J.J.'s wife and daughter were half-way across the country, visiting her family. Otherwise they all might be gone."

"But . . . you mean it wasn't spiders?"

"*Spiders?* Well, maybe in the sense that people were dropping like flies, I suppose."

I felt that pit beneath me grow deeper.

"Most people didn't know about the epidemic until it was all over," said Mrs. Pohl. "They kept it awful quiet. Still, I would have liked to have seen him one last time."

I offered her a smile. "Maybe you will someday."

She peered at me through her teary, unfocused eyes, unable to make out the details of my features. Then she turned away, put back the medal, and took down a photo album. She sat on the couch, and little Jason, who had torn down the foldout fence to get in the room, climbed up next to her as she opened the album. The kid pointed at a picture. "Ga-ga!" he said.

"Yes," said Mrs. Pohl. "You're right, that's Grandpa!"

He looked at me and laughed.

Mrs. Pohl turned the next page, as if she had momentarily forgotten we were there.

Paula cleared her throat. "Uh . . . Mrs. Pohl?"

She looked up at us, momentarily startled, and sighed. "You know, I don't feel much like bingo tonight," she said. Then she dug into her sweater pocket and held out a roll of dollar bills to Paula.

"Here," she said, "it's only right — you came all this way."

"No, you don't have to."

"Please," said Mrs. Pohl. "I want you to have it." When Paula didn't take it, she put it in my hands, and smiled, much happier now than when we had arrived. "Take her to Braum's, and get yourselves a couple of those giant banana splits," she said. "J.J. just loves banana splits!"

As she turned, I stopped her and said, "Oh, look — here are your glasses! They were on the mantel all along!" I handed them to her. "Here. You'll be able to see the pictures now."

"The mantel! Well, doesn't that just figure." She turned and headed for the couch. I was gone before she slipped the glasses on.

Paula didn't say a word to me as I walked her home. But then I didn't say a word to her, either. It was as if the sudden reality of J.J. Pohl came down between us like a soundproof wall. I wouldn't break up with her tonight. Even if tonight was the last night we ever saw each other, I refused to say those words.

Something was brewing inside of me now — something about Paula, and J.J. and Grant and my parents — and I knew if I wasn't careful, I'd have one of those moments where everything comes together. I wasn't ready for that.

As we neared her house, she stopped me by the curb. "Wait here," she said.

She went into her garage and came out a minute later, carrying a pick and a shovel. Somehow I didn't think we were going to use them for banana splits. She handed me the shovel and strode off down the street. I followed.

"What's this for?"

"First you tell me how a man who died seven years before you were born has your face."

"He doesn't have my face — I have his."

"And maybe you can tell me how you could look me in the

eye when Grant was feeding me that garbage about the spiders. I'll bet you all had a good laugh, didn't you?"

"I didn't laugh."

"Fine," she said. "Then maybe now you can tell me whether or not Ethan's alive."

This pit had no bottom; I knew that now. "I have no idea," I told her. What did it matter what I said now?

"Well, it's time we found out," she announced. "So we're going to the cemetery and dig up his grave."

In the cold moonlight, the graveyard was all blue monoliths and long black shadows. You'd think a graveyard would be a terrifying place at night — and it is when you're standing on the outside. But once you hop over that fence, you realize it's not much different from the land around it. Except of course for the dead people.

Ethan's grave looked much the same as it had two months earlier. Small plugs of ivy had been evenly spaced across the mound of dirt like a cheap hair transplant. There was no headstone yet, and it looked woefully lonely.

"Paula, this is crazy!" I insisted. "This is nuts!"

"So put me in a padded cell in the morning — but right now this is what we have to do." She looked at me as I held my shovel. "You start," she said.

The corner I was in couldn't have been any tighter. Either I dug, or I left and she did it by herself, which I felt she might just do. Paula could achieve just about anything, whether it was grandiose or depraved. I couldn't justify leaving her alone to do this, so I began to dig, hoping that she'd change her mind a few feet down.

I only dug the spade in once, then flung the dirt off to the side . . . and when I looked up, I saw a moonlit fist flying in my direction.

Bam! She threw a right hook to the jaw that practically spun my head around.

"You lousy, stinking, lying creep!"

There was only one possible response to that.

"Huh?"

"If there was any chance that Ethan was really down there," she said, "you wouldn't have gone anywhere *near* that grave, and you know it! You wouldn't even have come to the cemetery!"

She was right. It was a trick, she got me, and now I was dead.

"He's alive," she announced, "and you've known it all along, haven't you?"

"Uh . . . well . . ."

"Forget it," she said, taking my shovel, and her cap. "You've already given me your answer." Then she stormed off, leaving me standing over the empty grave.

I plodded my way back toward Old Town. By now they were probably wondering where I was, and I'd have to come up with a good story. More lies. My breakup with Paula had not been the clean surgical procedure it was supposed to be — it had turned into a chainsaw massacre, and the more I thought about it, the worse I felt. I kept thinking about what I had done to her and about how the lies got layered so thick, I could barely breathe. It would have been bad enough if I had done this to a stranger, but I had done it to someone I truly cared about.

The thought pulled out an intense flow of tears. Ethan had

said we could just cut the thoughts and feelings out, but I wasn't there yet, and I could not live with this.

I doubled back, racing at full speed, till I reached the graveyard, then continued on toward Paula's house, my superior lungs never getting tired, my superior legs never getting weak.

I reached her house and jumped over the fence, determined to tell her the truth a million times over until she believed it — but as I crossed the yard, I was intercepted by an unexpected countermeasure. Mookie.

The second he had smelled me, he bounded out of the doghouse. Without a single hesitation, he grabbed my leg in his powerful jaw and bit clear through my pants and into the flesh.

I yowled in pain and reached down, prying him loose, but he lunged again. And so I kicked him — forgetting how powerful my kick would be.

Mookie never stood a chance. He went flying over the doghouse and over the low-hanging moon, then landed in a patch of dense grass — and didn't move.

That's when I looked up to see Paula watching out of her window, her eyes gaping in horror.

I didn't mean it, I didn't mean it, I wanted to say, but the only thing that came out of my mouth was a desperate, mournful wail.

She screamed, and I bolted.

There were so many things that were beyond salvage now, and inside my head I heard Grant, and Ethan, and everyone else saying how I should put it out of my mind. *Just let it go,* their voices said. *It will all seem unimportant in a little while.* I cursed myself for not being able to be more like them and more like my parents, who had successfully put the past behind them, no matter how hard it might have been.

My mind was reeling — filled not only with thoughts of Paula, but of J.J., the stranger whose face I stole. And then I found myself thinking about all the strangers, in all the pinprick road-apple towns in the world that were exactly like Billington, people with no idea of the big surprise looming on the horizon. There must have been something seriously wrong with me, because all I could think of were them, instead of my friends in Old Town.

I looked down at my leg, which was spilling blood all over my sneaker, and suddenly a realization hit me that seemed more horrible than anything I could remember. In the dim moonlight, I couldn't even tell what color my blood was.

I was running with no destination, but my homing instinct brought me to my old house, the one I'd lived in when things were nice and normal. I had no key, so I kicked in the door with my good leg.

Inside, the house was much the same, less a few chairs and mattresses — but most everything else had been abandoned there, just as everything in Old Town had been abandoned so many years before. I sniffed the air. Mom and Dad had had the electricity turned off, but they hadn't emptied the refrigerator, and the stench of putrefied food filled the stagnant air like a disease.

I searched through the usual places for a flashlight, and when I found one, I took a deep breath and aimed it down. The blood was red. There was a lot of it, but it was red, and I could deal with that.

I bandaged my leg in the bathroom, then went into my parents' closet, not even knowing what I was searching for until I found it — and once I found it, I didn't even realize what I was about to do. It was as if I were outside of myself, watching it all happen.

I silently returned to the bathroom and pulled off my shirt. Then I turned the flashlight on my face and studied myself in the mirror. In the harsh contrasts of the light beam, I could see my change intensified. The delicate shape of my nose, the smooth cut of my cheekbones, the perfect curve of my chin, and that shimmering pelt of angel hair beginning to coat my shoulders.

Brutally beautiful, savagely Godlike, the stunning and perfect end product of Creation — so why did I find myself wondering if there could be such a thing as a monster with the face of a god?

I turned off the flashlight, and in the darkness, I plunged in the stinging hypodermic, pumping its thick pink liquid into the flesh of my half-human shoulder.

15

Bad Hair Day

There was no excuse for what I had done, and no one I could tell. The shame of having taken the old serum was a burden I would live with alone — and it would weigh on me every moment of every day in the compound.

Grant had promised there would be no more secrets between us, yet now I was the one keeping a secret. It would have been easier to live with if I had a clue as to why I had done it. Used to be, when I did things on the edge, I knew exactly why I was doing them. Most of the time it was just to be a nuisance. But this was different. I hadn't done it to defy anyone. I hadn't done it for the excitement, and I definitely hadn't done it to be unique. It served no practical purpose other than to make my life miserable.

It took a few days for me to realize what effect the shot would have. It didn't reverse the process of change, but it did stop it. It was like pouring water on a fire, and I found myself caught in a limbo of being half this and half that.

I tried to tell myself that it was good and that it would turn out to be the best thing for me, because maybe now my troubled thoughts could catch up with the changes my body had undergone. Then the next week, Doc Fuller would give me the good stuff again, and I'd pick up where I left off, just a week behind the others.

That's what I told myself.

But when Doc Fuller gave me the good stuff, I snuck right off and gave myself the old stuff once more. Two weeks, I told myself. I would only be two weeks behind the rest. Then I would be ready. But as that second week neared its end, I realized that I wasn't any more ready than I'd been before. My parents had hoarded plenty of the old serum back at the house, in the event of a quick escape. But what did using it buy me? I was just treading water.

And all this time, I led the others, encouraging them, calming their fears, telling them all about our big, bright, beautiful tomorrow, while secretly I was keeping myself from being a part of it.

And then my parents left.

It wasn't just mine — the adults had been shipping out daily now, ready to fulfill their roles as obedient little cogs in the clockwork of doom. Mine were the last to go, leaving behind Doc Fuller, Grant, and a meager handful of adults I didn't know.

I was alone in the barracks, trying to steel myself for another day of deceit among friends, when they came in to say good-bye. As had been the way of things lately, Dad kept his distance. Even Mom didn't get too close.

"I suppose when we see you again," said Mom, "we won't even recognize you. You'll have to tell us which one you are."

I could see she was holding back tears, and doing a good job of it. I'm glad, because I didn't need melodrama — and I know this is an awful thing to say, but I wanted them gone. I didn't want them to see me now, because if they looked too closely, they would see the shame and the lies in my face.

But they didn't look closely — in fact, they couldn't make eye contact with me at all. And in a way, that was worse.

"We're headed for Chicago," Dad told me. I already knew that much. The adults had been stationed pretty much around the world. Some in major cities to worm their way into computers and the economic infrastructure, whatever that was. Others went to small towns. Wesley's parents, for instance, had left a few days earlier; their glorious mission was to travel through small towns and round up people with psycho potential, who hated the government. This from a couple who used to free flies from flypaper.

Mom and Dad said their stilted good-byes to me. Then, just before they left, Dad turned and said something curious.

"Someday, son," he said in his best Ward Cleaver voice, "I hope you'll find a way to be proud of us . . . no matter what we do."

I thought it strange, because it seemed like something I wanted to say to him. It didn't make sense to me until much, much later.

The day after they left, I counteracted my third set of shots, and soon after, my spinning world fell off its axis and went completely out of control.

"It's brilliant," Ethan announced as he crunched on a piece of meat that was charred black — apparently the way he now liked it. "Tell them, Jason."

He was talking about The Plan. We were sitting in the diner

at twilight, and everyone wanted to know what the big plan was. It was part of the information that was supposed to funnel through me but hadn't been. I had sat in on enough meetings, but I couldn't bring myself to discuss it with the others.

Ethan sat on one side and Wesley on the other — the Trilogy of Terror reunited. But Wesley wasn't looking sociable. In fact, he looked about as morose as I'd ever seen him, as he swatted mosquitoes and pondered the Formica tabletop. He had been like this ever since his parents left. In fact, once our parents had started leaving, the invasion we all whispered about suddenly became very real. It hit Wesley hard.

"Yeah, Jason," said Wesley. "Tell us about the plan. I want to know what our parents are up to. I want to know how it's going to happen."

It was the end of a brutal day — four hours of glovecraft, followed by grueling endurance exercises that seemed designed for maximum pain. I was too exhausted to resist, so I sighed and spooned it out to them by rote. "Phase one," I said. "Cultural inflammation. We turn whole social groups against one another. Keep them hating; keep them divided. We take the worst side of human nature and use it against them."

One of the kids looked at me with wide blue eyes. "You mean we can *do* that?"

"It's kind of like acupuncture," I told him. "If you tweak the right pressure point, you can make people feel anything. I guess we've figured out ways of making it work with whole groups of people, too."

"Is that where our parents are going?" asked Wesley. "To tweak pressure points?"

I nodded but couldn't look him in the eye.

146

"It's great!" said Ethan. "They'll be so busy fighting each other, they'll never see us coming!" He rapped me in the arm. "Go on, tell them what's next."

"Phase two," I droned. "Foul the network. Hit every major computer system and corrupt so much information that the world economy begins to collapse."

"Ooh!" said a bunch of them, as though they were watching fireworks.

"Phone systems won't work," added Ethan excitedly. "Banks won't work. No one will be able to find out what's going on."

"Phase three," I said, pushing this last part out like a bad piece of meat. "Arrival. Keep them confused, keep them in the dark, and devastate them with a single blow so hard, they'll never recover."

"When?" someone asked.

"No one knows for sure," I told them. "We'll know when they get here."

"That's why we have to be ready," added Ethan.

And then I heard a voice across the diner.

"Will I have to kill anyone?" asked Ferrari. Everyone turned to look at him. "I don't want to kill anyone." I'm sure many others were thinking about that, too. I know I was.

While I was figuring out how I would answer, Billy Chambers answered for me, from across the room. "No sense worrying about things like that now," he said.

I began to feel an adrenaline fury replacing the exhaustion in my bones. "Why shouldn't we worry?" I turned to Ferrari, who, like so many others, had already graduated to the true weapon. "Look at that glove you've been wearing on your arm and wake up," I told him, and everyone else. "That thing doesn't have a stun setting — and if you think a weapon like that is for anything else but killing people, you're living in dreamland."

Ferrari recoiled, as if I had slapped him hard across the face.

"Grant says," Ethan firmly pointed out, "that we shouldn't think of them as real people, like us."

"It won't be so hard," suggested Roxanne. "If you can shoot them down on a video game, you're already halfway there."

Ferrari considered this. He didn't seem entirely convinced, but he was working on it. "I'm pretty good at video games," he offered.

I sat there, trying to process all of this. For the most part, these were my friends, but the things they were thinking. . . .

"It's like Jason says," Ethan reminded them. "It's *our* world now, and nothing else matters."

And I realized that whatever they were thinking, I had helped put in their heads.

I looked to Wesley, who was looking down at the table, still picking at the peeling Formica. Did he accept all of this? Had the doubt been washed out of his mind as well? Or was he just going along because he was told to? Like me. I wondered how far along we'd be willing to go.

"I think the plan stinks," I announced.

No one was expecting to hear that from me. Any other discussion in the room suddenly ground to a screeching halt. Then someone spoke up.

"Easy for you to say," said Billy Chambers, sneering. "You don't even have your real glove yet."

Billy smiled coldly at me. His homely features had been the first thing to go, and with his newfound good looks came a cruel arrogance.

Wesley jumped to my aid. "He doesn't have his real glove because he hasn't asked for it."

Billy crossed his arms. "So why haven't you asked for it?"

"Because I don't need to impress Roxanne," I told him.

Some of the other kids chuckled. I noticed that Billy was the only one in the room who actually had his glove on. It seemed that he always had it on. He moved his finger slightly, and it began to glow.

"While I'm in charge here, no one lights up inside," I warned him. "Turn it off, and put it away."

Billy glared at me but obeyed.

That's when Grant made his standard stealth appearance behind us, leaving me no way to know how much he had heard.

"Anyone up for a game of chess?"

"Jason doesn't like the plan," declared Roxanne, erasing any doubt as to what kind of evening this was going to be.

"I didn't say that."

"He said that it stinks," clarified Ferrari.

Grant raised an eyebrow but didn't miss a beat. "He's entitled to his opinion." Then he sat down facing me, crossing his legs like a talk-show host. "If you think you have something more effective, why don't you share it with us. Or better yet, why don't you get a message to your parents — I'm sure they'll be thrilled to have your input."

"I don't have anything better. I just don't think it has to be so cruel."

Grant gaped at me and laughed heartily. "Cruel? Us? No, never! In fact, it's one of the kindest things we can do!"

Even Wesley sat up and dared to question Grant now. "You think it's kind?"

149

"You've all heard of the expression *natural selection*, haven't you?" said Grant. *"Survival of the fittest?* Even here on earth, they've discovered that particular law of nature. All these years the people here thought they were at the top of the ladder, but soon they'll discover us, quite a few rungs above them. It's easy to survive when you're the dominant species — but let's see how well they do under us!" Grant gestured with a raised palm, as if offering something of great value. "Now they'll have the golden opportunity to *adapt.* They'll have a chance to evolve and grow once more — this time into something that serves *our* needs."

"And what happens if they can't adapt to living under us?" I asked.

"Then the kindest thing we can do is prevent their suffering." Grant casually pressed his thumb against his forearm, crushing a mosquito attempting to dine on him.

"Extinction," proclaimed Grant, "is one of the most perfect acts of justice the universe has to offer. Nothing becomes extinct that doesn't deserve it."

I could see everyone watching him, hanging on his words, and absorbing them into their own beliefs.

"Does any of this make sense to you?" asked Grant.

Agreements and affirmations filled the room. Some half-hearted, but too many were filled with deep conviction. And not a single voice would contradict him.

None but mine.

"No!" The word was out of my mouth before I knew I would say it. "No, it doesn't make sense. It sounds really good. It almost sounds wise — but that doesn't make it *true.*"

Grant leaned back in his chair and grinned. "Well," he

said, "lucky for us you're such an expert on truth, Master Miller."

There were a few chuckles, but most everyone was quiet, wondering where this would end.

"I'm not so good at truth," I told him, "but I know all about lies." I stared at him, refusing to break eye contact. It was a mistake — because he stared right back at me. Then the expression on his face changed. I could tell the moment he noticed that something was strange about me.

I stood up. "C'mon," I told everyone, "let's get back to the barracks."

And Grant said, "No. No, we'll all stay here for a while."

No one moved, and I realized that in a single sentence, Grant had taken away every last bit of my power over the Transitionals. If I stayed, I lost. If I left, I lost. And it dawned on me that my power was an illusion. I thought of Paula, and how in the end, I had dumped her — just as he wanted. I thought of that night in his garage, how he had taken our anger against him and turned it around, announcing that there would be no more secrets — as if it had all been his idea. Just as a magician misdirects his audience, Grant had used me to steal everyone's focus, in a smooth sleight of hand.

"Jason, could you take off your shirt?" he commanded.

I just stood there, not daring to do it. Everyone waited, wondering what new trick Grant was going to show them.

"Jason, please: your shirt."

"C'mon, Jason," said Ethan. "Take it off — what's the matter with you?" Ethan stared at me with his cold, inhuman eyes, and I knew that he had already shut me out. I had instantly been dismissed from his friendship.

151

Slowly I reached down and pulled my shirt up over my head. "There, are you happy?"

"Turn around, please," said Grant, and so I did. I turned a humiliating 360 for the group. Grant stood up and looked me over as if with a magnifying glass.

"Mr. Tyler," he said. Ty Tyler, the brawniest of us Transitionals, had been sprawled across the counter, yawning like a lion. When he heard his name, he sprung up and bounded to Grant's side.

"Yes, sir?"

"I want you to take Jason over to Doc Fuller immediately. I think something's gone wrong with his treatment."

Whispers from the group. Ty Tyler felt the fine fuzz on my shoulder, which was more than a quarter inch shorter than everyone else's. The look on his face was something between concern and disgust. "Yeah, sure, Mr. Grant."

As he escorted me out, I noticed Billy quietly take my seat beside Ethan.

As we walked down the weed-clogged pavement of our fenced-off camp, I felt like a convict being walked to the gas chamber. Although only my shirt was off, I felt completely exposed and vulnerable. A fine drizzle and an evening breeze made the hairs on my back and neck stand on end.

"Jason," said Ty as we approached the small house where Doc Fuller had set up shop, "if y'don't mind me saying so . . . I think you're a little touched in the head." He spun his index finger by his temple, in the universal Crazy Gesture. "I mean, look at us — we've all got it made! We got everything good comin' to us — the only ones in the world who do — and

152

you're talkin' like it's a curse. Well, you know what they say: You shouldn't kick a gift horse in the mouth, or something like that."

We reached Doc Fuller's, and the doctor said he could see me right away. He led me into his examining room while Ty waited outside, probably pondering facial kicks to gift horses. Doc Fuller's new office was an odd place. A little bit home-town family practitioner's, a little bit starship sick bay. Reflex mallets and stethoscopes were lined up next to holographic retinal scanners and microdiagnostic thingamabobs. I threw my shirt into a corner, put my training glove up on the sink, then hopped onto the examining table. The doctor glanced at the glove and at me, but said nothing about it. Still, I could tell how surprised he was to see that I, of all people, had not moved beyond the heavy metal monstrosity. The glove was a constant source of embarrassment for me, but even so, I knew that I didn't want the real thing. I've never been afraid to fire a weapon, but *that* kind of power did not belong at my fingertips. Or anyone else's for that matter.

He felt my underdeveloped back hairs and frowned. "You're not progressing," he mumbled. "That's odd."

Behind him, I heard the drip of what sounded like a leaky faucet. The door to his laboratory was open, and I caught sight of a light blue liquid flowing through tubes and distilling through a series of complex processes, until it came dripping down into a sealed flask: our new-and-improved serum. *Drip, drip, drip.* I could feel my anger powering up again. This kindly doctor, who had seen me through all my childhood diseases, was now brewing potions to turn kids into creatures. He should have been called Doc Frankenstein.

He looked down my throat, listened to my heart, scanned

my retinas, and asked me to cough. Then he asked, "Have you been feeling strange in any way, Jason?"

"Yeah," I told him. "I've been feeling like an alien."

He ignored my answer. "Stomachaches? Shortness of breath?"

I shook my head. *Drip, drip, drip.* The sound from the laboratory was like a water torture. The fear and fury of a trapped animal flowed through me, mounting with every drip of the serum distillery.

The doctor opened a drawer, pulling out a hypodermic and some empty blood vials. "We'll analyze your blood samples, figure out what's wrong, and raise your serum dosage. We'll have you caught up with your friends in no time." He smiled and wrapped a rubber tube around my arm. "Make a fist."

As he dabbed my bulging vein with alcohol, I realized that I was not going to let this man put another needle into my body. With my free hand, I knocked the hypodermic to the ground.

He snapped his eyes to me, suddenly realizing how desperate I was. Before he could say a word, I took my conveniently fisted hand and swung it across his jaw. He flew backward into his instrument shelf, knocked out with a single blow. The shelf, and Doc Fuller, came clattering down in a cacophony of metal and glass. I wanted to destroy the serum distillery, too, but Ty burst into the room.

"Hey, what gives?"

With no time to lose, I grabbed my glove and hurled myself into Ty, whose bulky frame gave just enough for me to push past him. Then I tore out the front door, into a growing downpour.

"Hey! Stop!" he yelled. "Somebody stop him!"

Even through the rain, his voice rang as loud as a siren, and the Loyal Order of Transitionals spilled out of the diner like a swarm of bees from a hive. They spotted me instantly, and to my horror they were right between me and the gate. I saw the glow of several gloves beginning to power up. Did they mean to kill me? Had their allegiance changed so quickly — one minute I was their leader, and the next minute I was the hunted? If Grant now saw me as a threat, he could order them to catch me dead or alive. Some of them might not fire — but I knew a few who would.

I charged into a home and turned right, down one of the connecting corridors that I had helped to build, through another building, then down another corridor. I pushed through the deserted homes that our parents had occupied for such a short time, turning this way and that in the maze of the compound, until I found myself in a dark, derelict home that had not yet been reclaimed from decay. I was at the edge of the compound. The shouts outside grew as the hunt intensified.

Thinking quickly, I put on my clumsy metal glove and went to a broken window. In the middle of the street, I could see Grant giving orders and Billy repeating them. I took aim at a window across the street, cocked my finger, and let loose a single shot. The window shattered, and drew everyone's attention.

"Over there!" shouted Billy, and they all ran to the home across the way.

I turned, preparing to head out the back door, but someone was there, standing in my path, glove powered up. I gasped — and then in a moment I realized who it was. It was Wesley.

"Wes, thank God it's you!" I said. "Listen, we gotta get out of here."

Wesley powered down his glove but didn't move.

"Come on!" I insisted. "Don't you get it? I'm asking you to come with me!"

"But what's the point? Where could we go?"

"Anywhere!" I told him, with growing frustration at his boneheaded lack of momentum. We should have been gone by now! "I've got tons of the old serum — we don't have to become like Ethan! *We don't have to be one of them!*"

"But — Grant —"

"To hell with Grant!" I shouted in a loud whisper. "He doesn't own us."

Wesley considered that, then said weakly, "I think maybe he does."

I didn't expect that from Wes, but then, lately my friend had lost his former predictability. "Wes, *please!*" I begged. "Haven't you figured out what they are? Is that what you want to be?"

Wesley shifted his weight from foot to foot. "It doesn't matter what I *want* to be. . . ."

"We can fight them!" I told him. "We're the only ones who can — but first we have to get out!"

Wes just kept shaking his head, as if trying to wake up from a bad dream.

"I was wrong," I admitted. "This world *doesn't* belong to us — to them. They have no right to come here and steal it!"

"I know," he finally declared. "And I know I should go with you — but the thing is —" Wesley swallowed hard. I could hear the tears in his voice, although I couldn't see his eyes. "The

156

thing is, I'm not like you, Jason. I'll never *be* like you. I'm not that strong."

I heard footsteps on wood again, drawing nearer.

"I'm sorry," he said. Then he turned and shouted down the dark corridor. "I found him! He's in here!"

An icy tightness grabbed my gut. I had no words for this betrayal — nothing I could say to Wesley now — and no time even if I found the words. I took off, running past him, just as the others burst into the room. I wanted to hate Wes for what he had done, but I was too terrified to feel anything else.

"There he is!" yelled a voice that I knew was Billy's. The room glowed with the fire of his weapon.

I burst out the back door, tumbled down the steps and into the dense weeds.

The fence was before me now. I leapt onto it and scaled it at full speed, then flipped myself over the top, but my pants snagged on a barb, leaving me to hang there like one of the scarecrows in target practice.

I turned to see Billy, his face wet from the rain. In his hardened expression, I could see that his limited conscience had been killed by weeks of Grant's rhetoric. He took aim.

"No!" I swung my arm up in a futile attempt to block, and the blast hit my training glove. Pain exploded from my right arm as I broke free of the fence and fell to the ground.

With pain searing up and down my arm, and Wesley's betrayal still churning in my gut, I forced my will into my legs and ran. I refused to look back, not daring to see if they were behind me. Tree limbs whipped at my face and shirtless body, until I came out into the fields beyond Old Town. My feet padded through mud and grass, leaving a trail, but the rain was coming down so hard now, I hoped it would wash away my traces. Just to be sure, I leapt into a creek and followed it for almost half a mile before daring to climb up to the other bank.

My arm was screaming in pain, and I knew I had to go somewhere to take care of it, but where could I go that they wouldn't look for me? Only one safe haven that they wouldn't think of came to mind.

Knowing that Grant and the others might spot me on roads, I ran over pastures and through gullies, until I came to the neighborhood I was looking for. Drenched to the bone, I jumped over a low fence and collapsed in pain at a kitchen door, then pounded my good fist against it.

In the light coming from inside, I could see my arm now. The intricately built glove, full of chambers, tubes, and precision mechanisms, was now a fused mass of metal. The entire glove had melted onto my arm. Its metal fingertips had peeled back, revealing painful red fingers. It looked like a steel cast.

The door opened, and the old woman gasped. "My Lord! What's happened to you?"

"Mrs. Pohl," I said, "I need your help."

She peered at me, this time wearing her thick glasses, and suddenly grabbed the doorframe, to keep herself from falling down.

"J.J.?" she said, bewilderment shooting through every synapse of her brain. "J.J., is that you?" I could see her fighting to make sense of me. "Is that you, J.J.?" In the end, I think her mind chose to protect itself by shutting down a few breakers. She began to act as if this were part of a much longer dream. "But . . . but they told me you were dead."

I didn't know which was worse — to shatter the dream or play along. "Yes, and no," I told her.

"Well, you come right inside!" she insisted. "You'll catch your death of cold dressed like that." She helped me up and brought me into her warm, flower-scented home.

Once inside, she dug out some boy's clothes that must have been forty years old, from a dresser that must have been filled with things of J.J.'s she refused to throw out. Then she gently cleaned off my fingers and poured alcohol down my metallic cast — which hurt something awful but not as much as I'd thought it would. She asked what happened, and I told her it was something that happened in the war. Then she cooked me a thing called a Monte Cristo sandwich, "With lots of powdered sugar, just the way you like it."

Every once in a while, she'd be clipped by a moment of clarity and turn to me, asking, "Who are you, really?"

"Jason Jonathan," I would tell her, which was, in fact, true.

She'd accept the answer, and the moment of clarity would meander away. "Would you like to watch Ed Sullivan? It's Sunday, don'cha know."

As the evening went on, the pain in my arm faded to a dull throb and the tightness in my gut receded. I found myself relaxing, feeling safe, at least for the moment.

As I lay on the couch, Mrs. Pohl sat in a brightly patterned armchair with her Bible, something I imagined was probably a daily ritual. She noticed me noticing her. "Would you like for me to read it to you?" she asked. "Like I used to when you were little?"

"Yeah," I said, and then added, "How about the one about the guy who gets eaten by a whale?"

"That'll be Jonah," she reminded me. "And it's not a whale — it's a 'great fish.' "

She found the Book of Jonah and began to read in a quiet, soothing voice. Behind her voice, I could hear the breeze giving life to a wind chime and further beyond that, a million creatures sang to the night, with the last few raindrops of the storm. I took a deep breath of the home's flowery air, picking out the scents of rose petals and jasmine. And on the wall, I noticed a silly old Norman Rockwell print, which I recognized from my parents' coffee-table book. It was a corny thing of a scrawny, nameless kid with his arm around an equally nameless girl with pigtails. I smiled broadly. How dumb, I thought, but still let my eyes slowly pore over its subdued, earthy colors. . . .

And for a few suspended moments, I was able to trick myself into feeling human. It was a simple state of being that was so incredibly joyful, I wished I could live in the moment forever, sandwiched between the geeky kid and his girlfriend, between the wind chime and rosy air, between the ceiling and floor of a small house, in a small town, in the middle of nowhere special.

16

Ballistic Dawn

I don't remember my dreams that night, but I know they were the first good dreams in a long, long time. I *must* have been crazy, and this was proof, because in the darkest moment of the worst nightmare of my life, I had found contentment sleeping on an old woman's couch.

I awoke that morning to the sweet smell of pancakes cooking, and an early morning tranquility. In that brief moment of pre-wakefulness, I couldn't recall exactly who or where I was — and that was okay. Unfortunately my sleep-induced amnesia was shattered by urgent knocking at the front door. Everything came rushing back to me, and I groaned, realizing that nothing had ended. This early morning visitor had to be for me; no one knocked like that for a gentle woman like Mrs. Pohl. My arm still throbbed dully, my stomach still rolled in waves of distress, and my will to run had not yet woken up.

The door rattled one more time before Mrs. Pohl hurried to answer it. She was not happy about this intrusion — any intrusion was a threat to the fragile fantasy I had given her.

"Who are you?" she said suspiciously as she opened the door. "What do you want here? Are you friends of J.J.'s?"

Then I heard a voice I was not expecting.

"You remember me, don't you, Mrs. Pohl? I'm Paula. I baby-sat for you."

I sat up and brought my knees up to my chest.

"J.J.'s not seeing visitors right now," said the old woman, "so you just get along."

"Please, Mrs. Pohl, if Jason's here, we need to talk to him."

We? I thought. Who was "we"?

I had my answer in a moment. Paula and Ferrari stepped into the room. I didn't dare imagine what conspiracy of intrigue had brought the two of them together. Mrs. Pohl eyed us with great concern, then left for the kitchen to deal with pancakes and escape this encounter. There was no such escape for me.

"I've been looking for you everywhere," Ferrari informed me, and he explained how he finally asked Paula to help. It was Paula who suggested I might be here. I looked at Paula, but she seemed so guarded, I couldn't read how she felt about all of this.

"Jason, you've gotta come back right away," begged Ferrari.

"I'd rather have my head melted off," I told him.

"But you *have* to!" he insisted. Although Ferrari didn't have that air of arrogance most of the others had been developing, he had never looked this rabbit-scared, either. "You have to, on account of Wesley," he said.

The mention of his name brought too many mixed feelings for me to sort out just then. "What about Wesley?"

"He went totally ballistic in the middle of the night,"

explained Ferrari. "Now he's holed himself up in the —
uh" — he glanced at Paula — "in the . . . *storm cellar,* and he
shoots at anyone who tries to come near him."

The hairs on my neck stood up so sharply, it hurt.

"Exactly which storm cellar do you mean?"

"You know . . . ," he prompted. "*The* storm cellar."

I stood up. There was no mistaking what Ferrari was talking
about. What was Wesley thinking? What was he doing down
there? I glanced at Paula, who was taking all this in but asking
no questions.

"We're really scared, Jason. Grant just paces and yells orders,
and Billy keeps pushing people around, but nobody knows
what to do."

I could imagine them there. Only a handful of adults
remained, leaving mainly us Transitionals. With Grant and
Billy in charge, I dreaded to think of how it might end.

"There's one more thing," Ferrari said, his words catching in
his throat. He glanced at Paula, and then I guess he just gave
up trying to keep secrets. "It's Ethan," said Ferrari. "He's dead.
For real this time."

I forced myself to take a deep breath, but it came out in tight
staccato beats. My God, what had gone on there, while I slept
so peacefully? I knew I couldn't ask with Paula there.

"Has anyone contacted my father?" I asked.

Ferrari shook his head. "I heard Grant talking to Doc
Fuller — they haven't showed up in Chicago yet. I don't think
things are going the way they're supposed to."

I felt the sickness in my stomach again but beat it away. I
didn't dare consider what might have gone wrong. I turned to

Paula, who stood a step beyond the room's threshold, as far away as she could get. I longed to reach out to her, but I had no clue how to bridge the distance.

"Okay," I said to Ferrari, "you go ahead. I'll catch up with you."

"You promise?"

"I'll be there."

Ferrari looked at me, worried, then left.

Paula took a step forward, but only one step. I didn't know what to say, so I said the first thing that came to mind.

"I'm sorry about Mookie," I told her.

"Me, too," she said. "I guess if he attacked me, I would have kicked him away, too." She started rubbing her arms as if it were cold, although it wasn't. "I went to your house a few days later but couldn't find you. Then, when we heard that everyone at Holy Circle Nondenominational had actually moved into Old Town, my parents made me stay away. I almost did sneak down there to check it out, but I got kind of scared."

I grinned feebly. "You? Scared?"

"Well," she said, "I figured that if it was worth lying to me about, maybe it was worth getting scared about, too." She glanced at the pictures of J.J. Pohl on the wall behind me, comparing them to my face again, then said, "You know . . . Ferrari really doesn't look right. He looks a little too . . . *healthy.* I guess it's more than just good nutrition, huh?"

No matter what, I wouldn't lie to her again. "Do you believe in aliens?" I asked her.

She brushed back her hair, trying to pretend that the question didn't trouble her. "Should I?" she asked.

And very softly, I said, "Yeah."

From the next room, Mrs. Pohl called out cheerily, "Priscilla, dear, would you and your little friend like blueberry pancakes, too?"

I took a few steps closer to Paula. I was glad that she didn't back away. "Could you stay with her for a little while?" I asked. "Tell her I had to go away again, but that it was good to be here one last time. I think she'll understand."

Paula looked down, wringing her hands, but then forced herself to look me in the eye. "Will she see you again?" she asked.

I wanted to tell her yes but couldn't bring myself to do it. "I don't know," I answered.

School counselors had always pegged me as being just a little bit self-destructive, but I never thought I'd be so self-destructive as to race back to Camp Old Town the day after I almost died there. It had to do with that problem of living with myself again. If I didn't do something about Wesley, I knew it would haunt me for the rest of my life, however long or short that might be.

I caught up with Ferrari, and we walked through the gate together. The status of things had not changed much from what he had told me. A bruised Doc Fuller and several more adults stood in the street, and the Transitionals meandered while Grant paced. Every once in a while, someone who apparently thought they could have a rational conversation with Wesley descended the moss-covered steps of the storm cellar, only to emerge a few minutes later, looking terrified and relieved, as though they felt lucky to have escaped with their lives. This was not the Wesley I remembered. He might have been a maniac, but he'd never been homicidal.

As the others saw me approach, they all took notice, either standing straighter or turning away. When Billy saw me, he made sure to stand directly in my path.

"The traitor returns," he said.

I wouldn't justify him with a comment. "Tell Grant I'm here."

But Grant had already seen me and approached. It was actually worth coming back, just to see him this powerless.

"You should know," he said with no love in his voice, "that you brought this about. I hold you responsible for everything that happened here, and you will be dealt with accordingly."

"Threatening me's kind of counterproductive, Mr. Grant. Don't you agree, Billy?"

Billy sneered, but I could tell that he was squirming.

I grinned. "Now I may have to ask both of you to get down on your knees and beg me to talk to Wesley."

Mr. Grant just shook his head. "You're a very disturbed boy, Jason."

I laughed out loud at that. This show was definitely worth the price of admission. I'll admit I was terrified, but suddenly I realized that I didn't care that I was terrified. If I turned around and left, Grant lost. If I went down there and talked sense into Wesley, Grant lost. No matter what he did to me, it wouldn't change that simple fact, and he knew it.

"Okay, I'll make a deal with you," I told him. "If I get Wesley out of there, you let us both leave and you pretend we never existed. If I can't get him out, then you can 'deal with me accordingly.'"

"Deal," he said, far too quickly. I knew he was lying — it was obvious that honor was not valued among the "superior." Still, I had chosen to come here, regardless of the consequences. I supposed that meant I would die with my integrity. I turned and walked down the steps of the storm cellar, into the darkness of the buried ship.

It was the first time I had been down there since that night with my father. I expected it to somehow feel different after all I had been through, but it still struck me the same way: a cold, uninviting shell that spoke of nothing familiar. I paused only for a moment to look into the room where my father had reminded me of the Warrior-Fools. The places where we'd sat still remained as clean spots in the dust. I tried to imagine riding in a craft like this to a home I had never seen, with the strange and beautiful people that I would have nothing in common with but the form of my flesh. If that was my destiny, then destiny had no soul.

I pushed deeper into the ship, through the dim light that filled the gray corridors. I could hear a sound now. A faint vibration that came from far below. A throbbing hum that resonated in my throbbing stomach.

A corridor up ahead was riddled with holes like a wedge of Swiss cheese, and I saw red light coming from a room dead ahead. All of the holes except for one were melted in the metal of the ship. The last hole had found a different target.

Ethan's lifeless body lay sprawled ungracefully across the floor. I could imagine him coming down here, filled with faith in his superior mind and body, so sure he was too special to die in such a sad, sorry way.

I forced my eyes forward and stepped over Ethan's body, refusing to look at it. Ethan was right. You can push some things out of your mind when you have to.

My steel cast accidentally banged into the wall with a loud clang, and in an instant I heard holes sizzling into the walls around me.

"Wesley, don't! It's Jason."

The firing stopped immediately. I didn't dare move until I heard him speak. His voice was close, but his mind sounded far, far away.

"They caught you," he said. "I knew they would. I knew they would."

I ventured forward. "No," I told him. "I came back by myself. Because I heard you went schizo. Of course, I told them it wasn't possible — first you have to *have* a mind before you can lose it."

I thought it might get him to laugh, but it didn't. Grant was right; this was my fault, at least partially. With all the strange things taking root in our heads lately, I supposed I had mulched something into Wesley the night before that sort of cracked his planter. There was so much about it that made me feel awful, and yet in the midst of the grief and dread, I felt a glimmer of something good as I slowly stepped into the room. Perhaps it was just a strange ricochet of shock.

I realized right away that this room was the ship's bridge — a small, cramped place, not at all what I'd expected. There were three seats before a viewport that now viewed nothing but dirt.

Beneath the viewport, the navigational console was turned on. It was a computer screen as wide as a tabletop and full of open computer windows. Each window was filled with either unreadable hieroglyphics or incongruous graphics. I wondered how anyone could hope to navigate with so much input to consider.

There were three seats in front of the console. Two of them were occupied. In one sat a skeleton, an unlucky traveler who hadn't survived the violent landing twenty-two years before. It occurred to me that burying the dead must have been a human extravagance. I'd have to ask my parents about it if I ever saw them again.

In the other seat was Wesley.

"So," I said to him, "do you think Gleeb over here will mind if I sit with you guys?"

Wes glanced at the slouching skeleton. "Gleeb doesn't mind," he said. "I think maybe Gleeb wants to take Ethan's place in the Trilogy of Terror."

I felt a wave of sorrow hit me at the mention of Ethan. I tried to tell myself that I had lived through his death before, but it made no difference.

I sat down in the third seat. "What happened, Wes?"

"Did you know," he said, "that they have this same navigational console set up inside a pair of V.R. goggles? It's true. That's what I do for six hours a day. I sit and trek the stars and never have to leave the little room. Sometimes I get to blow things up, too."

He reached down and, touching the screen, dragged a few of the computer windows to different places. Then he touched one with his thumb. The faint vibration of the ship grew a bit louder.

"Purrs like a kitten," he said. "You think maybe I could trade it in for a Porsche?"

I leaned closer to him. "You gotta know that this is serious, Wesley."

He turned to me. "I didn't mean to hurt Ethan!" he shouted. "But I did, and now there's nothing I can do about it!" He looked at his gloved hand in rage. "There's no safety on these things. There's not even a trigger. You barely even think of moving a finger, and the thing goes off. You try to scratch your nose, and you wind up with no head."

"Somehow," I said, "I don't think that the ones who made it really cared who or how many people it killed. Just as long as it killed."

He ripped the weapon from his hand and threw it to the ground. "What are we, anyway?" he asked, looking at his own body, halfway to perfection. "I mean, what kind of screwed-up trick of evolution makes us look so incredible and then makes us the assholes of the universe?"

"I think you've figured it out," I told him. "It *is* a trick. Think about it — can you imagine what an army would do when they first saw us coming? They'd be so awed just by looking at us, they'd forget to be afraid. They'd start believing that they deserve to lose."

I realized I was avoiding the heart of my mission. "Wes, why did you come down here?"

"Did you know," he said, slapping a tear out of his eye, "that my parents didn't even stop in to see me when they left? They told Grant to tell me good-bye. Does that stink, or what?"

"It stinks. Why did you come down?"

Wes considered the console before him. He knew I wasn't going to let him change the subject again. "Don't you see, Jason — you *mean* something. You could go out there and prob-

170

ably win half of them over. I'll bet you could get them to hurl Grant off a cliff if you tried hard enough, and Grant knows it — that's why he had to wipe the floor with you. But I don't mean anything — not even to my parents. No one listens to me. No one ever has; no one ever will. I could never do a thing about Grant, or Billy, or the ten gazillion ships whenever they get here. And then I start thinking, Maybe I *can* do something that makes a difference. Can you imagine what'll happen if I take this ship out of here? Everyone'll see it. It'll be like skywriting across the world that we're here!"

I shook my head. "How could that make a difference?"

Wesley turned to the console with even greater resolve. "We'll just have to find out."

I was getting more and more worried for him now. "Wes, this thing is badly damaged. If you try to start it, it'll just blow up and kill all of us!"

Wesley nodded, and moved his fingers across the face of the console. "That works, too."

The vibration became a violent rattle, and a high-pitched whine screamed in my ears. The dirt in front of the window shifted. "It's just like the simulator!" he said.

"Wesley, don't do this!"

"Too late," he said. "I've started the launch sequence."

I grabbed his arm. "We're getting out of here!"

"Go if you want," he said. "I don't care."

But I did care. I looked at my metal cast. It wasn't much of a weapon anymore, but it was still good for something. I raised it high into the air and brought the thing down on top of Wesley's head as hard as I could. In an instant he became as limp as Gleeb. Either I had killed him or knocked him out, but I couldn't worry about it now. With my good arm, I pulled him out of the seat and hoisted his dense, half-alien mass over my shoulder, racing back the way I had come, saying a silent final good-bye to Ethan as I passed him. There were strange, blaring sounds now, and I realized that warning alarms must sound the same in any world.

With all my strength, I ran down the long corridor, into the storm cellar, and up the stairs into the unbearably bright light of day.

Grant was right there.

"What's going on? What have you done?"

"He started the launch sequence."

The fear in Grant's face turned to panic. "And you didn't turn it off?"

"Sorry," I said. "Wasn't in my training."

Grant let out a defeated whine and hurled himself down into the dark hole.

The ground was shaking like an earthquake now. Everyone was scattering, racing out through the gate and scaling the fences. Not even Billy bothered to harass me — he pushed smaller kids out of his way as he fled.

Behind me I could hear a loud crack as the ruined foundation in front of the cellar split apart. My heart leapt with terror but also powerful anticipation — because I knew that Wesley was right. Everything was about to change again, and whatever happened now, it *would* make a difference!

You can't imagine how different tomorrow will be!

I burst out through the gate and tore through the woods, hoping I could get far enough away. The pain in my gut exploded into my arms and legs as I ran with Wesley's impossibly heavy body on my back, but dropping him was not an option. Neither was slowing down. Ten seconds. Fifteen. The groan of the malfunctioning engine became a violent scream behind me. Twenty. I burst out of the trees and into a field. A flash of light, and a shock wave hit my back, knocking me down. I heard the roar above my head now, and as I looked into the sky, I could see it!

It rose huge and black against the morning sky, molting a trail of crumbling earth behind it. The ship was inelegant and cumbersome — an ugly thing nowhere near as exquisite as the creatures it once carried. I could imagine Grant in there now, at the console, trying futilely to control the thing, but as it corkscrewed into the sky, I could see that an entire engine had been crushed and a second one torn away.

Wesley, still alive, opened his eyes and caught sight of it. "Ooh!" he said weakly.

The ruined ship reached its peak half a mile up — high enough for everyone in Billington to see. Then it slowed — and stopped, hanging in the sky for an instant before it began to fall straight down, back toward Old Town.

It gained speed as it plummeted, its crippled engine sputtering, wind whistling around it. I grabbed Wesley again, dragged him forward toward a gully, and hurled us both down into the ditch as the ship disappeared beneath the treetops.

This, I now knew, was the *real* focal point of our lives. Either it would be the most important moment we'd ever have — or it would be the last.

The sky turned white, and the blast shook the dirt of the gully down around us, covering us in layers of wet earth. Then came a second blast so powerful, it filled the gully with the shredded limbs of trees that had been a hundred yards away. Finally the ground stopped shaking, but my ears rang on for a long, long time.

Wesley looked at me, semiconscious, his eyes half open. "Did I do it?" he asked. "What happened?"

I brushed the dirt from his face and laughed, suddenly feeling freer than I'd ever felt before. "Damned if you didn't skywrite the world!"

The winds of change are definitely not a warm summer breeze. They're more like tornadoes. You never know when they're coming, and they tend to turn everything upside down. I'd been dragged by a powerful change all summer, but the moment that ship exploded, I knew that the tornado had died — and although a new one was swirling in to take its place, I had a feeling I'd be able to ride this one, rather than letting it ride me.

Down in the ditch, Wesley and I were covered in Billington dust — the same red-brown dirt that clogged the treads of my sneakers and got swept to the corners of my room for my entire life. Now it coated me like a second skin, but I no longer found it a nuisance. In fact I took a deep breath, getting a full dose of its earthy aroma, before I had to cough it all back out.

As I helped Wesley out of the ditch, I turned to look behind us. Through the mangled foliage and settling dust, I could see the smoldering ruins of the ship and of Old Town. From here it seemed that not a building of the compound remained.

In the fields around us, others who had hit the ground when

the ship blew up were just getting to their feet. I only saw the Transitionals and wondered if the few remaining adults had been able to put enough distance between themselves and the blast. They were not graced with the same powerful stride we had all developed. Even with Wesley on my back, I had outrun them.

The Transitionals were like a school of fish now, scattered by the passage of something far mightier. Only now were they beginning to drift back together as they regained their bearings, and in spite of everything, when they saw me, they began to move in my direction, as if I were the core of what bound them together. If they thought I could give them answers and direction, they were wrong. This was a task I could no longer perform. I had to be one of them to lead them, but I was firmly on the outside of the group now. No matter how the coming days unraveled, I knew I could never truly be one of them again.

Perhaps that's why Billy decided to kill me.

"Billy, no!" Wesley shouted, but he was still too weak to stand up and stop him.

Billy rammed into me from behind, sending me sprawling on the ground. When I looked up, I was staring at the business end of his glowing index finger. As the others saw what was about to happen, they hurried, but none were close enough to stop it.

"I could waste you with a single finger," he said, flooded by the power of the thought. In his own mind, he was justified — he would be ridding the ranks of a dangerous traitor. But this was different from last night — he wasn't firing at a shape in the dark; we were point-blank, looking into each other's eyes. I could tell by the look on his face the moment he had crossed the line and decided to really do it.

But I think that when he realized he had crossed that line, the last remnants of his conscience stumbled on it. The enormity of the act struck him with such astonishment that he hesitated — and in that moment of hesitation, something else struck him as well.

A rock.

It flew in from nowhere and smashed his nose like a meteor impacting on the moon.

"Strike!" said a voice far behind me. It was Paula! Never had I been so glad to hear her voice.

Billy's whole body flinched wildly from the blow, his glowing arm suddenly firing in all directions. I jumped up, grabbed his pinky, and twisted it, forcing his weapon to power down, then tore the glove from his hands. He fell to his knees, completely forgetting his role as executioner, and gripped his gushing nose, wailing in pain.

In the commotion more weapons had powered up around us — Roxanne had arrived, and the second she saw the source of Billy's pain, trained her glove on Paula. In turn, Ferrari aimed his at Roxanne, to stop her from firing. In an instant, it escalated out of control — a dozen terrified Transitionals, not even knowing where they were aiming, or why, brandished their weapons in a sort of random standoff. We were all about to be part of a massacre.

"Power down!" someone shouted. The voice was loud. It commanded authority.

It was Wesley.

Still reeling from his blow to the head, he stood on shaky legs and proclaimed to the jittery crowd, "What are you, a bunch of idiots? Power down, and take those damned things off!"

One by one the gloves turned off and were shoved into pockets with great relief. Wesley turned to me, shaking his head. "That was so stupid!" he said. "*I've* never even been that stupid."

Paula came up to me, offered a quick smile, then knelt down to help Roxanne attend to Billy, whose wailing had subsided into whimpering. Roxanne eyed Paula coldly but, to her credit, didn't push her away.

"You know, Billy," said Paula, "I liked you more when you were ugly on the *outside*." But she said it with such compassion, it gave him pause for thought. He looked at her from above his bloody nose, then at me. I think in some strange way, he was just the tiniest bit grateful that Paula had broken his nose before he could kill me. He'd probably hate us till the end of time, but at least he wouldn't have to go to sleep that night a killer.

More Transitionals came drifting in from farther away, but not a single one of the adults. Someone suggested that we go back and try to find them, but we knew it would be foolhardy and futile. Old Town was engulfed in flames, the entire compound quickly burning to the ground.

"Maybe we'd better bail, before people start showing up and asking questions," suggested Wesley.

It was right about then that my stomachache came back. It had never completely left, but with everything going on, I had forced myself not to deal with it. This time the dull ache exploded into searing pain that I could not ignore. It caught me by surprise and I doubled over, feeling myself go weak at the knees.

"Jason, what's wrong?" said Paula.

"Someone shot him!" I heard one of the others say.

But there was no hole. No damage. This was something else. I stumbled away, gasping for air. My mind was so fouled with pain, I couldn't think what the problem might be.

"We have to get you to a doctor," said Paula, "both you and Billy."

"What doctor?" asked Ferrari.

It was a question with too many ramifications. Doc Fuller hadn't made it out of Old Town, and our parents had scattered themselves around the globe. We were suddenly very much alone in the world.

I collapsed to the ground as the pain multiplied, spreading throughout my body. An indescribable agony. It felt like . . . It felt like . . .

It feels like appendicitis.

I opened my mouth to speak, but nothing came out but a bloodcurdling scream. And then another, and another. Helpless, I could see the others over me in panic, but I couldn't hear them through my own screams. Even Billy had stood up and was looking down at me in disbelief. If he had suggested putting me out of my misery, I would have been the first to agree. I instinctively knew that, whatever this battle was, I could not possibly win. I was dying — and nothing could stop it.

So I locked my eyes on Paula's, determined to keep her face with me as I was dragged kicking and screaming into the darkness.

And then I died.

17

Starborn

There was no funeral.

There were no mournful friends.

There was nothing but water. I was drowning in a glass of water.

"Swallow, Jason. Swallow. . . . Good."

The water tasted cool and sweet on my parched lips. I opened my eyes and saw nothing but a round opening before me, pouring more water down my throat. I coughed and gagged.

"Is he awake?"

"He's starting to come around."

The voices were familiar. I took another gulp of water. This time my throat muscles did what they were supposed to do.

I tried to put my thoughts in order, but it was like bobbing for apples. I couldn't get my teeth into a single coherent thought and was afraid that if I couldn't find one soon, I'd slip back into the void.

Finally I found a thought that I could cling onto.

These were my parents.

I was grateful to know this, but I also knew that my parents should not be here. They were supposed to be somewhere else. Where were they supposed to be?

"Chicago," I said, my voice sounding like gravel in a sieve.

My eyes came into focus, and I saw my mother smile. It was the first time I had seen her smile since the good old boring days. "Forget Chicago," she said.

All at once, the eventful summer began to flood in on me, starting with Grant and the glove, then the compound, then the explosion, then winking out of existence while staring at Paula's face.

"How long?" I asked.

"Almost a week," Dad said. Which surprised me — I was sure I must have been out of it longer, considering how awful I felt.

I had no clue where I was. It wasn't home; it wasn't anyone's house I knew. And I was lying on a soft fur rug.

For an instant I thought that the ships might have arrived while I vegetated and perhaps I was aboard one of them — but it was nothing so spectacular. The glass of water I was drinking from said HOLIDAY INN. I smiled. How gloriously unexciting.

"You made a real mess of things in Billington," said my father. "It was on the news, the tabloids — even the respectable papers were running stories about aliens."

I could see great disappointment in both of their faces. "Sorry I couldn't be the son you wanted."

My mother turned away to wipe tears from her eyes. And my father sadly shook his head in shame. "It's our fault," Dad said. "If we had seen how you really felt about things, we would have made you a part of what we were planning."

"I *was* a part," I reminded them. "I was at the meetings —"

Mom gripped my hand. "No, we mean what your father and I were planning."

Dad sighed. "We thought you'd be ashamed of us — that you'd turn us in if you knew we meant to sabotage our own scheme."

I stared at them in dim disbelief, but rather than stuttering whats, whos, hows, and wheres, I took the glass from my mother, drank the water, and listened. They told me how it had been — how all the others shifted quickly into reverse and denied their twenty years of being human the moment Grant announced that he had received his fuzzy transmission. Better to side with the stronger team, I suppose. Much more convenient. It's funny how convenience can sometimes knock out conscience in the first round.

"We couldn't let Grant run the show," Dad told me, "so we pulled rank and took over our old roles."

"We'd always been trustworthy," Mom added. "So no one suspected what we were really up to."

I sat up and grinned. "What a bunch of traitors we turned out to be!" And then, when I glanced at the bed, I noticed something odd.

There was no fur rug down there.

When the truth dawned on me, it came in such a violent rush that I began to shake. I closed my eyes and let it sink in. I must have known all along but refused to let myself consider it. Even before I had slipped out of consciousness in the field, I had felt things changing inside of me — the penalty for trying to counteract the serum. Now I took a few deep breaths, held up my hand in front of me, and opened my eyes.

My skin was the color of perfect peach marble.

"Mom!"

They both reached out to grab me, as if I would go into convulsions.

"There was nothing we could do," they told me. "By the time we heard about the explosion and came home, it had already happened." They told me about how Paula and Wesley sat by my side, hidden in our garage, terrified that I might die. Then they told of how all the Transitionals fled when the investigators started to show up. Even Wesley had to make a quick exit.

"They left Billington, and no one knows where they've gone."

I thought about them all out there. Without the benefit of Doc Fuller, they would finish their transition the same way I had finished mine. Although I doubted theirs would be as bad, since they were so much further along than me. Without a means of finding their parents, they would stick together — they *had* to — hiding from the world until the ships finally came, tomorrow or in ten years. They would survive, but what a humbling experience it would be.

I slowly stood up, then went into the bathroom and raised my eyes to the mirror, to see what looked back at me. A strange and perfect face, gossamer hair like diamond thread — I was a thing of unimaginable splendor. Then a tear came to the corner of my intense blue eyes. Because more than anything else, I wanted to be J.J. Pohl.

Mom brushed a hand across my soft shoulder. "You'll grow used to it," she said in her comforting way, "but life is going to be very different for us from now on."

"Can you ever turn me back?" I asked.

Dad shook his head sadly. "Not after what you've been through. And even if we could, that DNA no longer exists. The human part of you is gone forever."

I gazed at my exotic, unfamiliar image in the mirror, and in spite of everything, I didn't feel all that bad. Maybe because I knew that in a very important way, my father was wrong.

A few days later, my parents drove me on a three-hour trek at my request. Paula came along. To be honest, I might not have had the courage to go without her.

"I told my parents I'd bring you home for dinner if they let me go," she told me. I didn't know whether her parents were extremely cool or just morons. But somehow I didn't think morons could give rise to someone like Paula.

Halfway through the trip, she asked me why I kept looking out of the window. "What do you see out there?" she said.

I shrugged. "Just what's there."

"You're so weird now," she said, and I knew she wasn't talking about my face. It was the way I sniffed the air when we rode past a field of flowers, the way I held my hand out to feel the pressure of the wind in my palm, and the way I stared at everything from barns to bicycles as we passed. It had nothing to do with the way I looked, but everything to do with *me*.

We arrived, and the others left the car first. It took a moment for me to build up the nerve. As I stepped from the car into the busy street, people backed away. Some laughed at first, as if it must have been some gag, but when they took a good look at me, they knew I was the genuine article. Their eyes showed a strange mix of fear and amazement, which must have been how I had looked when I'd first seen Ethan.

"What's the matter," Paula scoffed at them, "you have a problem with extraterrestrials?"

The four of us walked side by side as we mounted the many steps of the state capitol, my parents standing as proud as I've ever seen them. Seas of people parted for us. A few took pictures, but their hands shook so much, I can't imagine they'd be in focus. Still, I smiled for them. It all made me think of the time in sixth grade when I painted a green streak in the middle of my hair just to be different. Some kids just shook their heads; others came in the next day with streaks they had painted in their own hair, impressed by whatever statement I was making. Today, too, was a day to make a statement.

"I'm afraid there won't be any glory," my mom had said. "History isn't kind to traitors."

"That depends on whose history you read," I told her.

At the entrance to the state senate, where the governor was delivering an address, a guard gripped his gun in mortal terror as he saw us. Then, as I got closer, he just dropped all of his defenses and stared in wonder. That was part of the problem we needed to fix.

"We would like to address the legislature," said my father.

The guard just shook his head and stammered, "But — but —"

I took a step toward him. "Please."

I suppose the magic word worked, because he reached for the brass knobs of the high double doors and swung them wide. Inside, a booming voice echoed a speech about taxes and budget to the huge crowd. I took a deep breath. Warning the world had to start somewhere. This was as good a place as any.

"Are you sure you want this, Jason?" my mom asked as people inside began to take notice.

I nodded. "More than anything."

The awestruck guard couldn't stop staring. "Who are you?" he dared to ask. "*What* are you?" I answered him only with a smile as wide as the space between stars. Then I strode forward, down the red-carpeted aisle, proud amid the gasps and confusion, never letting that smile fall from my face.

Sometimes we make our alliances not by the shape and color of our flesh but by the convictions of our heart. I know that Wesley, Ferrari, and all the others will have to find peace with themselves very soon — but as for me, you could say that my ship has already arrived. Because no matter what my reflection tells me — no matter what genes give rise to my form — I know exactly who and what I am.

I am Jason Jonathan Miller. And I am human.